THE GOLDEN CEILING

A JEFF TAYLOR MYSTERY

Also by Scott Lipanovich

The Lost Coast

THE GOLDEN CEILING

A JEFF TAYLOR MYSTERY

Scott Lipanovich

Encircle Publications
Farmington, Maine, U.S.A.

Editor: Cynthia Brackett-Vincent
Cover design by Christopher Wait
Cover photgraph © Getty Images

Published by:

Encircle Publications
PO Box 187
Farmington, ME 04938

info@encirclepub.com
http://encirclepub.com

For K.I., whose every step contains joy.

PART ONE

One
_____

During the summer between my second and third years of medical school, in Sacramento, I took an internship. The plan was to spend three days a week in the pediatrics ward, transitioning into the clinical work of the next year. In the spring I'd been considerably impressed with a lecture given by Bruce Fisher, M.D. He agreed to let me intern under him, and offered use of his hospital office as a home base during July and August.

On my second day, while looking over a patient's chart, the office door swung inward. A tall, gaunt, quite older man entered and quickly took the chair opposite the desk where I sat. His face threw off chalky light. Shaggy white hair draped his ears. The man's posture was notable for his age, steady as a flagpole. Wearing a worn gray T-shirt, jeans, and beat-up work boots, he looked like one of those people you see in photographs from the Dust Bowl. Deep wrinkles crossed his forehead and marked his neck. Hazel eyes seemed to float in their sockets, as though they didn't require earthly attachment. They glowed like those of a preacher about to commence speaking in tongues.

A knobby right arm shot forward. "The safe is not safe. But the ceiling at heaven is golden."

I rose from my chair. He rose as well. I motioned for the old fellow to remain seated. "How can I help you?"

Again, the knobby arm shot ahead. "My name is Clyde."

"Are you okay, Clyde?"

He nodded, then shook his head. The long white hair brushed his ears. "I am fine. The safe is not safe."

I looked through the open doorway, expecting an attendant to arrive at any second. "I understand. How can I help?"

His chin dropped. He slumped. As if in apology, his face squeezed together. "I am lost."

"Let's see if we can get you found. Do you know where you were last?" I came around the desk. "Or maybe you have something with your name on it."

The man's face brightened. "I do!"

He stood, beaming, fished a wallet out of a back pocket and thrust it toward me. The wallet's scarred brown leather appeared to have been stitched together in the last century. Just as I was about to open it, another man came into the office. Unshaven, his cheeks and short hair a grizzled gray, he looked to be in his sixties, a good two decades younger than Clyde. Thick everywhere but the gut, you could see he'd done hard labor for most of his life. His skin resembled the old brown leather wallet.

The man said, "Here you are. You scared the hell out of me."

I said, "Can I take it you two are together?"

"I bring him in for radiation once a week. While we're waiting, I go get a drink of water and he vamooses on me."

I looked to the older of the two. "True?"

Again, the sheepish face. "I'm not sure."

I handed the wallet back. Clyde took it with both hands. He wrapped fingers around my chopped, disfigured right hand. A blissful smile lighted pale cheeks. "I see you're among the chosen."

Clyde plopped onto the chair. He seemed utterly content. I don't think he had any idea of where he was.

The other man said, "Hal Bell here. Thanks for looking after my buddy." He didn't offer to shake hands. I was used to it. Bell turned, touched the old guy's shoulder. "Come on, Clyde. They're waiting for you."

Hal Bell led Clyde out of the office. I returned to the patient's chart. Eleven years old, she had been running a low fever for eight days. We did blood work. Nothing. She didn't have the flu or a cold. Normal in every way except the persistent fever. Cases like this were more interesting to me than the cases I'd worked in my previous job, being a snoop at Sherman Investigations, a well-connected detective agency three blocks from the capitol building in downtown Sacramento.

I studied more charts and made notes in the hospital's computer. Due to join Dr. Fisher in making his afternoon rounds in pediatrics, I headed out. On the carpet was the scuffed wallet. Clyde must have missed the pocket when putting it back. I picked up the wallet, caught a musty smell reminiscent of old books, slipped it into the back pocket of my slacks. I headed out to drop it at Hospital Security, in another wing of the sprawling concrete and glass medical center. Running late, I decided to drop it off after rounds. I only remembered the wallet while driving home, when I felt two lumps in my back pockets.

Once home, I opened the wallet. The nosiness I'd cultivated working at Sherman Investigations kicked in. Again, I received the musty book smell. Inside was a driver's license, expired, showing a younger and better-groomed Clyde, whose surname was Whitney. According to the license he lived on Red Corral Road, near Pine Grove. That's a small town in the foothills, established during the famous Gold Rush of 1849. Also in the wallet were Whitney's Medicare card, a separate card for United Health Care, and an Amador County library card—everything dirt streaked. Ones, tens and twenties lined the billfold. Tucked in the seam behind the billfold was a small Ziploc baggy half filled with gold dust.

Also, a square of paper. In tidy printing: *If found, please call 916-537-7347. (If someone finds Grandpa and he's lost.)*

Rather than call the number, I fired up my laptop. I searched: *Clyde Whitney, Pine Grove, CA*. Those glowing holy-roller preacher's eyes, his intense sincerity, and the gold dust stirred my inquisitive impulses. I'd make the call and arrange for return of the wallet, but first I was curious if I could learn anything about old Mr. Whitney. Because of his age—the driver's license birthdate put him at eighty-eight—I thought little of his life would be found on the internet.

Wrong. MIT grad Clyde Tuohy Whitney was a legendary innovator in the early days of weather satellites. Some of his work had been for the government, and secret. At turning sixty-five, articles in sources as varied as *Science News* and the *New York Times* reported on the "Godfather of Weather Forecasting" walking away from the industry at its zenith. His wife had recently died of pancreatic cancer. In interviews, Whitney told reporters that after her death he was turning his life's focus to recovering gold unearthed during the Gold Rush, but too minuscule to retrieve through the mining techniques of the time. It simply floated away when whole hillsides were blasted down to rock via crude hydraulic mining. Asked how he would achieve this, Whitney merely smiled. The articles described him as viewing gold in close to mystical terms. He sold one of his patents and bought a house seven miles from Pine Grove, and bought the nearby, long-shuttered Watters Mine. The last bit of Clyde Whitney information I found was in *Gold and Treasure Hunter Magazine*. A reporter tried and failed to get Whitney to discuss his plans for an island he'd purchased at the confluence of the Feather and Sacramento Rivers, roughly a triangle of flat land perched above winter flooding. That reporter also cited a mystical view of gold held by Clyde T. Whitney.

After that fun diversion, I called the number placed inside the wallet. A woman answered with a simple hello. Her voice was as clear as the handwriting on the square of paper.

I said, "My name is Jeff Taylor. I'm calling regarding Clyde Whitney."

"What? I just saw him an hour ago."

"Actually, I'm calling about his wallet. I found it today at the UC Med Center."

I heard a slight sigh. "You had me worried for a second. As you can see by the note, sometimes he gets lost."

I described Clyde wandering into the office. Explained I was doing a medical school internship at the hospital, thinking it might make her more comfortable. I told her about the baggy of gold dust.

"I'm thinking I shouldn't leave the wallet at Hospital Security, not with this much gold in it." I looked at the Ziploc baggy and guessed it contained three ounces. "Feel free to search for Jeff Taylor on the medical center's website."

This brought a chuckle.

"Did I say something funny?"

"It's just that I'm already looking at your profile."

The more I heard the soothing rise and fall of her voice, the more I wanted to return the wallet in person. Her voice was not especially musical, yet it hummed along in an easy-going manner that triggered a warm feeling inside. "I could just drop it at the front door. That way I'd know it won't get messed with."

"I'm not worried," she said. "By the way, I'm Karen Brady. Clyde Whitney's my grandfather."

"Nice to meet you, so to speak."

Karen said, "If Grandpa discovers he's lost his wallet, or if I tell him about it, it might shake him up. Could you possibly bring it over? Is that asking too much? I'll have a surprise for you."

Now I was the one who chuckled. "A surprise for me? We've never even met."

"Do you have a pen handy?"

Two

The address Karen Brady gave me was a few miles beyond Sacramento's suburban sprawl, twenty miles from the little brick house I rented downtown. Crystal Meadows is high-end real estate. Parcels tend to run a full acre. Houses have abundant stonework in front yards, swimming pools in most backyards. They are almost all stucco, differentiated largely by color. The streets are squeaky clean.

Still hot out at seven p.m., I found open wrought-iron gates at 3134 Ralston Avenue. Pavement leading to the buildings was more a private lane than a mere driveway. This parcel was huge, about three acres. I approached a series of flesh-colored stucco buildings with red tile roofs. The general feel was Hacienda California Style. The main house, three stories, displayed none of the bold vivid colors, architectural detailing, none of the charm of a true Mexican family compound. I parked my veteran blue Volkswagen Jetta, and climbed out. Walking toward a front door painted the same red as the tile roofs, muffled voices came from around the left side of the house. Two people stepped into sunlight. Hal Bell, the second Dust Bowl man of early afternoon, exchanged gruff words with a short, solid-looking blonde woman. Her blue eyes slashed the air between them. I placed her in her thirties.

Crossing in front of the house, they noticed me. Bell took off a cowboy hat. They flashed reflexive smiles.

7

"I'm here to see Karen Brady. She's expecting me."

Bell murmured something to the woman I couldn't make out, then said, "Good to make your acquaintance again." He replaced the mushroom-colored cowboy hat. He walked toward a mammoth garage. Its four doors were open. Bell disappeared inside. Neither he nor the woman said the word goodbye. It seemed odd Bell didn't ask how I came to be there. I decided not to mention finding gold dust in Clyde Whitney's frayed wallet.

The woman spoke with an Eastern European accent. "Come on the porch, for the shade. I get Miss Brady."

The wide front steps and porch were of spotless reddish pink Saltillo tiles. Rather than colorful ceramic pots, to both sides of the bottom step were steel tubs sprouting prickly pear cacti. I passed between them to the shade of the porch. Looking down the long driveway, the open space between houses in Crystal Meadows suggested country living without the labor of rural life. Expecting her to come through the front door, Karen Brady surprised me by appearing to my right. A bit older than my twenty-eight years, she stood with the same superb posture as her grandfather, and like Clyde was a tall wiry blade. Chestnut hair, in a ponytail, rode capable shoulders. She had soft green eyes, a calm smile. She wore a sleeveless blue top, hemmed cut-off jeans and rope sandals.

We exchanged hellos. I kept my mangled right hand hidden in a front pocket of my work slacks.

Karen said, "Let's go back to my place. I'm warming up the planet by keeping the house cool."

Karen seemed about five feet nine. No makeup. No earrings or jewelry of any kind. There I was, compiling mental notes about someone, like I did when making reports for Sherman Investigations. Maybe once a snoop, always a snoop.

We proceeded along a cement path tinted a faint mauve,

between the oversized garage and the oversized house. Karen didn't move up and down as she walked; she glided. Passing a set of windows, the blonde woman I'd seen earlier stood at a sink. She quickly looked down. To the right beyond the main house were three round glass tables followed by a swimming pool. After that, a tennis court with lights for evening play. Left, well behind the garage, was a guesthouse. Then I saw another guesthouse, set in the back right corner of the property. That one had a garden of granite boulders and disciplined bushes. Over it loomed what in the Sacramento Valley is referred to as a Heritage Oak, a thick-limbed beauty at least fifty feet tall and two hundred years old. It stood out as the only tree on the ample property. Every place else had been altered. Every place else had been conquered.

Karen glided along. Although I'm six-three, I found myself picking up my pace to stay even.

She said, "Any trouble finding the place?"

"Not with Google Maps as my guide."

"Thanks for bringing Grandpa's wallet."

The guesthouse, coated with the same flesh-colored stucco as the rest of the buildings, was larger than my brick bungalow. Karen opened the door, waved me in. Instant coolness. A maroon couch, with an oak coffee table in front of it, faced a fireplace of rosy tiles. The fireplace did not have a screen or a log rack. Its mantel was empty. At both ends of the coffee table were upholstered chairs that matched the couch. I sat in one.

Karen said, "I made iced tea. Tell me, do you get used to the heat around here? I've only been here since mid-June."

She left the room. Her voice was, without doubt, East Coast.

I called into the adjacent kitchen. "It took me a couple years. I grew up in the redwoods, way up the north coast. It's usually cool but not really cold. Some of the freshest air in the country."

"Let me know if you bottled some. I could use it these days."

"I left it to come to the big city. But it's still there. Anybody can have all they want."

I looked around. Other than books and binders, and notes neatly printed on index cards spread across the coffee table, nothing indicated someone lived there. The white walls were naked. I set Clyde Whitney's wallet on the coffee table. I heard, but couldn't locate, a softly thrumming air conditioner. I checked out what were clearly class notes. They were of a medical nature.

Karen returned, carrying a glass pitcher and two glass tumblers. She set them on a corner of the low coffee table. She transferred books and papers to a walnut table in the adjacent dining area. She came back, and poured. She looked to the wallet.

I said, "Aren't you going to check inside?"

"Of course not." Karen grinned. "Wait—do I need to?"

I shook my head. I had trouble relaxing around her. Karen Brady had no trouble relaxing around me. Sitting on the couch, she exuded a quiet confidence.

I said, "I want to guess your accent. I say you're from Connecticut. Maybe Rhode Island."

"Pretty close. Go west into upstate New York. Rhinebeck."

"What brings you to California?"

This time her smile broadened to reveal splendid white teeth. She swung her chestnut ponytail off her shoulders. "You just ruined my surprise. I came to Sacramento for a master's in nursing, at the UC Med Center. There's an accelerated program that started in June."

"No way."

"Yes way. I'm studying elder care."

Karen reached around and re-planted her ponytail between lean shoulders. I picked up the wallet and flipped it open. No reaction from Karen regarding my half-hand. I slid out the plastic packet.

"I checked the price of gold. I'm guessing there's at least six thousand dollars' worth in here."

Karen said, "Grandpa loves his gold all right. He has more faith in gold than in people."

I didn't mention my pre-drive research. "I'd be happy to return the wallet in person. He's—well, he is an interesting guy. Me returning it might give him a little more faith in others."

Karen said, "He wouldn't remember you. He might even think you stole it. I'll slip it into his place. He'll find it and not remember losing it. Grandpa's staying in the other guesthouse, while getting his treatments. Did he tell you about that?"

"His friend Hal did."

At hearing the name, Karen frowned. She looked down at the wallet and baggy of gold dust. "Ask Grandpa about something that happened thirty years ago, he's got a photographic memory. Ask him about thirty minutes ago, he just stares into space."

"I'm sorry to hear it."

"It breaks my heart." Karen's face grew darker. This time her frown produced a set of faint lines above the eyebrows. "He was a world class thinker. Now he doesn't know what day of the week it is."

We picked up iced tea and stared into space ourselves. What could I say about her grandfather's dementia that wouldn't sound superficial, or condescending? We downed the iced tea in silence. Karen plainly didn't need to punctuate the quiet with chatter, which struck me as another indication of her confidence. I told Karen it was nice to meet her and headed into summer heat that reminded me of a swamp.

Holding onto the open door, Karen said, "Maybe we'll bump into each other at school." She didn't flash a smile. She didn't flirt.

11

I said, "I hope so."

I put out my trashed right hand. Karen shook it devoid of the hesitation I almost always get when someone touches its strangeness. Feeling like a dumb high school kid with a crush on a classmate, I headed for my car. The woman I figured was a housekeeper did the looking-down routine when I passed the kitchen windows. I took a gander at the imposing, sterile compound. I'd been too nervous to make good conversation. I'd learned almost nothing about lovely Karen Brady. I assumed she was family to whoever owned the compound, because of the Grandpa Clyde connection. That was about all I knew, other than she was in the graduate nursing program at the University of California Medical Center.

I opened the door to my car. Giving the place a final look, I detected movement in the shadows of the big garage.

Three

The first person to call me doctor was Jimmy McKinney. Six years old, he'd been limping after taking a fall on his bike. I was years away from being a doctor, but to a boy that young anyone tall and wearing a white lab coat seemed one. His face a fierce splattering of freckles, Jimmy looked from Dr. Fisher to me, and said, "Doctor Jeff, what happened to your hand?"

"It was an accident. I'm fine now. Thanks for asking."

During the summer after graduating from Sacramento State, working the evening shift during the tomato harvest, I'd lost the two smallest fingers of my right hand to a loading machine. And my middle finger, sliced in half, no longer rose to the occasion of flipping someone the bird. Performing the same rote task thousands of times, night after night, I'd slipped into daydreaming.

The injury hurled me into a downward spiral of self-pity and despair. I withdrew from medical school in Seattle, which I was scheduled to begin in August. How could I become a pediatrician, my life's goal? I'd scare the hell out of the kids. Drinking nightly and arguing with college basketball teammates—who tried to help me—I was without work, money, without hope. An older alum, an ex-Sacramento State basketball player himself, Clint Sherman, threw me a lifeline. Clint's private investigative shop was a favorite among political people, and wealthy people who wanted to stay

13

under the radar. The job paid the bills. I drifted in it for three years. Then my life changed again. In the process of solving a murder, I nearly got killed. This served as a wake-up call. My existence was month-to-month, with nothing meaningful developing. I quit snooping and took a car trip across the country. As more than three years had passed since taking the Medical College Admissions Test, I was required to take it again.

Starting medical school gave me purpose. Still, I was lonely. A loner since the hand slicing six years prior, my social life was virtually non-existent. Most of the guys I'd played basketball with had gone onto graduate school elsewhere, or found jobs in other cities. I didn't know how to make new friends. The night after meeting Karen Brady, I stretched back on the living room couch, took a slow breath, like before taking a shot from the foul line on a basketball court, and clicked the number I'd called the day before.

That effortless voice answered. "Don't tell me you found more gold."

"You're a mind reader. This morning I found two chunks the size of golf balls."

"Do you want to buy them? I'll give you a super deal."

"I wouldn't want to deprive your grandfather of his prized possessions." In my head I saw Karen's clear face, her easy smile. I said, "I'd take a reward though."

"Have anything in mind?"

"Are you up for a walk on Saturday? There are good hiking trails out your way."

"How about if I text you my email address? Tell me where and what time. I'll let you know."

I chose a paved trail along the North Fork of the American River, shortly before its waters spread into Folsom Lake. I'd jogged that path and thought it a good place for a walking date.

I emailed Karen about it, and suggested we meet on Saturday at eleven-thirty.

She didn't reply until the next morning: *Okay Taylor. You're on.*

Already ninety degrees out, I found parking under the partial shade of a lime-green digger pine. I wore a blue T-shirt, khaki shorts, and running shoes. An orange San Francisco Giants baseball cap protected my head of short brown hair, which of late I'd noticed was thinning in front. Heat waves shimmered above asphalt.

I glimpsed Karen from the side. She was looking at a sign with dotted lines, a map of local trails. She wore a marvelous straw hat with a long bill in front and a short one in back. A modest green day pack covered much of her ponytail. Her arms shined in bold midday light.

I offered Karen my bad hand. "I hope you're not as nervous as I am."

Karen said, "I'll take that as a compliment."

We headed toward a procession of oak trees. Karen's tennis shoes made pleasant skimming sounds across the paved trail. The baking air was still. It smelled of summer-bleached grass. We left the paved path and walked along a dirt one above the bluish river. We didn't see other hikers. We talked and sneaked glances at each other. The day grew ever hotter, blanching the sky. Dark circles spread from my armpits. Considering her earlier comment about Sacramento Valley heat, Karen didn't seem much bothered by it. Perhaps it's more accurate to note she seemed at peace.

We entered a passageway of branches—and came upon a coyote, its body hunched, its front legs bent. Karen and I froze. The coyote sensed us and looked our way. Its nostrils flared.

My hand touched Karen above her day pack. I said, "Let's stay still."

"Are we scared?"

I whispered, "Don't even think it."

The coyote's snout swung back. It pounced and came up with a wriggling green snake captured between clenched teeth. The coyote trotted off. A bit unsettled, we walked on. We rejoined the main trail. Soon we reached restrooms. I said I needed to go inside. Karen tucked into the women's.

Giddy from the heat and whitened sky, the adrenaline rush after surprising the coyote and the scent of Karen's warm skin, I peeled off my shirt and khaki shorts. I turned them inside-out for airing, and draped them over the metal partition of the toilet stall. We were separated by a wall of concrete blocks, open air above it for ventilation.

I said, "Give me a couple of minutes, okay?"

"Take as long as you need."

At the sink I filled my palms with cool water, and splashed my face. I cranked out paper towel and patted my sweating body.

I said, "I don't know how to tell you this, but I'm pretty much naked over here."

Karen said, "You're not."

"I am. I'm sweating like a pig. Whose dumb idea was it to go for a walk in this heat?"

"The same person who takes off his clothes on a first date."

I churned out paper towel and patted sweat off of my body again. While doing this I experienced déjà vu. I remembered doing everything I did, as I did it, each swipe of paper towel, running a paper wad under the faucet and applying it to my face. It was as if I were living within a movie I'd seen so many times I knew the details of what came next. The strangest part was experiencing the present felt like something I'd done eons ago. The only other time I'd experienced déjà vu was when I almost got killed, battling a murderer who himself was murdered minutes thereafter. I bent over, overwhelmed by chemical latrine odors, the recurring déjà vu, and emotions I could not categorize.

On the other side of the wall, I heard water splashing, then paper towel being cranked out.

Karen said, "That coyote and the snake, it was fast."

"Right now, everything's fast. You make me dizzy."

"I bet you say that to all the girls."

Somewhat refreshed, we continued walking. The path took us to a bluff that ran parallel with the river. My nervousness never abated. Words flew from my mouth. I told Karen about my mom getting pregnant, nineteen years old, unmarried, rejected by her parents and moving in with a friend in Grantsville, far up the cool northern California coast. I talked about playing sports and how that shaped me. I told Karen that living under the redwoods the air was so fresh it held a distinct flavor. I told her about slicing my hand. And that other than developing a friendship with Clint Sherman, a father figure, I'd treaded water those years working for his detective agency.

"Am I making a fool of myself, talking so much?"

"Better you than me." Karen gave my arm a friendly elbow bump. "Just kidding. Your stories tell me about you."

We headed back. We seemed to float on heat and conversation. We returned to the parking lot. Three gauzy hours had passed since meeting. My arms were sunburned. My shirt clung to me with warm sweat. I walked Karen to her car. We extended hands, to shake, and both went in for a kiss so swiftly our teeth clacked.

I said, "You taste familiar. Like from a long time ago."

Karen stepped back. She examined me. "You're different."

"Yeah," I said, "but I'm used to it."

The flavor of Karen's lips stayed on mine. Halfway home, the taste began to dissipate. I ran my tongue over her taste, savoring the last of it. The moment Karen's flavor was gone, I craved it. Images of our walk ricocheted around my brain. Getting off the freeway downtown, I was wound tight, driving hot streets fast. Huge sycamore trees, their branches making an overhead tunnel, created splotchy shadows that seemed to jump off the pavement.

Though I wasn't much of a drinker anymore, once home I poured a hefty glass of red wine and tried to settle down. Everything with Karen had come naturally, with warmth and vitality. The instinctive feeling of affinity that fizzed inside during our walk bloomed into elation.

I thought I heard Karen call my name from across the house. I hurried that way. Of course, she wasn't there. I regained equilibrium.

I spoke aloud. "That was one hell of a first date."

I forced myself to wait until seven o'clock before texting her. Afraid of coming across as too eager, I kept it brief. *Thank you for a great day. I felt drunk every time you smiled. Shall we repeat?*

The two hours I waited for a reply seemed far longer. I tried reading. The mind continuously circled back to Karen, until my phone let me know a message had arrived.

Right back to you with the thanks. Maybe I will get used to the heat after all. How about lunch tomorrow? If you're okay with it, your place would be great... I want to hire you. I'll explain. Send me your address. If you're game I'll meet you at noon with lots of food... KB

Karen Brady wanted to hire me? My mind had already leaped to thoughts of romance. Here she was suggesting I work for her. Doing what?

Rather than lose my cool and reply quickly, asking what she was talking about, I waited an hour, sent her my street address, and left it at that. Besides, she could have been joking.

Four

Karen's voice was as steady as her posture. It didn't rise and fall in tone; it marched forward. "They're all after it. Every one of them."

"And you?"

"I just want our fair share. It'd be my mom's fair share, and my aunt's. Grandpa has three kids, Aunt Lila, my mom, Caroline, and Uncle Stan. He's the little brother who has taken over everything. Most of the family lives in the East."

"Stan, and I'll assume he has a wife, owns the compound?"

Karen nodded. "He *thinks* he owns everything that's Grandpa's. I don't want him, or maybe Grandpa's sidekick Hal, to find a major stash and not tell anyone. Which is what I'm sure they'd do."

We sat at my kitchen table, four-by-five feet of solid Danish teakwood picked up on Craigslist. My only prized possession. It was covered with Thai food takeout boxes in various stages of being emptied. The food was good, the conversation confusing. Karen claimed everyone in her grandfather's orbit was scheming to find a cache of gold dust he was thought to have accumulated over the previous twenty years. She offered no evidence of the rumored fortune. She presented no evidence of a conspiracy by someone to find the gold, yet she spoke with utter certainty on the matter.

19

"Can I assume the baggy was in the wallet when you returned it?"

Karen jabbed her chopsticks at me, reminiscent of her grandfather's rapid arm movements. "I wouldn't steal from a stranger, let alone my own grandfather. What's wrong with you?"

I crunched an empty takeout carton, and went to the recycling bucket under the sink. I dropped the carton in. "You say you want to hire me to look into these people, when I was thinking more along the lines of dating. That's what's wrong with me."

I returned to the table. Karen reached back and centered her ponytail. "I only want what's fair."

"I could put you in touch with the place I used to work. They're pros."

Karen set down the chopsticks. Both hands dropped below the tabletop. Her face spawned a thoughtful frown. "Even though I don't really know you, I feel I can trust you. More than a total stranger. I have a feeling what happened to your hand gives you more empathy than most of us."

Karen's chin rose. Her eyes settled on mine.

I said, "Let's talk it through. No promises."

Karen described coming West every Christmas after Clyde bought the gold mine and the river island. Grandpa Clyde always gave each grandchild a mini packet of gold dust. "They were wrapped with notes advising us to do things like look at one blade of grass at a time, never a whole lawn. Or to walk in bare feet on dirt, to be one with the earth. Grandpa was quirky, but he was great."

I was on the lookout for a false note, an exaggerated gesture, something that seemed untrue: nothing of the kind.

Karen said, "He was always a little reclusive, but my mom says it was only after Gram died it became extreme. About three years ago, the dementia started up." Karen took her ponytail, pulled it around and pressed it to her lips. "Uncle Stan plans on building a boating resort on the island Grandpa bought when I was about eleven. He's got power of attorney." Karen tossed the ponytail behind her. "You see? I think he's planning to find Grandpa's gold and using it for the resort. God. There are so many cans of worms to open, I don't know where to start."

I said, "Let's start with Hal Bell."

Sherman Investigations kept three non-descript sedans for tail jobs. Since Hal Bell had seen my faded blue Jetta at the Whitney compound, if I were going to follow him I'd need an automotive disguise. The company cars were outfitted with binoculars, disposable gloves so you don't leave finger-prints when digging deeper somewhere than the law permits, that kind of stuff. Plus a CarScout, a tracking device you attach under a back fender that allows you to follow a vehicle with your phone.

Clint Sherman, sitting behind a large mahogany desk with family pictures at the front corners, nodded and rocked while I spoke. Bald, tall and lean, he was a person who viewed retiring as a sign of weakness. At times he tipped his face up and back, and peered through trifocals. I got his motor cranking when offering to pay for use of a sedan.

His froggy voice, coarsened by years of Scotch and when younger, cigars, came fast. "That's the most ridiculous thing I've ever heard. You know where to get the keys."

Clint stood. That meant the conversation was over. He said, "You didn't say a word about fee. I know that look. Your eyes are really on the young lady. Let me say," Clint added, "it's about damn time."

The next evening I went to Karen's. She told me Bell was having dinner with Clyde at the other guesthouse, beyond the swimming pool and tennis court. She described Bell's dented Toyota pickup, which he parked in the big garage to avoid the boiling sun. I clamped the CarScout under the back fender. This brought an uptick in my pulse I remembered from my snooping days. I downloaded the app to my phone. After that, it was only a matter of waiting for the phone to ping me. When I couldn't follow Bell—usually the case—the CarScout would store the pickup's every movement for later review.

During the week I learned Bell's patterns. Nights he parked at a residence in an unincorporated rural district fifteen miles east of my place downtown. Bell took two trips to the Whitney compound. On the second, he proceeded to the medical center. When he didn't go to Crystal Meadows he drove into the foothills, which people generally called Gold Country. It didn't take big-time sleuthing to find that Bell held two mining claims upriver from Clyde Whitney's Watters Mine. He shopped at a Safeway. He visited a rock and gem store in the town of Jackson. County records showed a dissolution of marriage to an Anna Carter Rogers, recorded in 2015. I found his contractor's license number, and a business license issued in his name for Bell Construction.

Saturday morning, I read the newspaper and waited for the now-familiar ring tone of the CarScout app. It came. I texted Karen: *Here we go.* Her *Thanks* was instant. I grabbed a notebook, camera, a bag of snacks and a bottle of mineral water. Though Bell was fifteen miles away, with the CarScout there was little worry of losing him. Traffic was light. I drove fast though not precariously.

Out of the city, I took rural Highway 16 through dry grasslands and valley oak country, then passed about a mile of vineyards. I reached an area known as Sloughhouse. Bell, well ahead, turned south onto Highway 49, narrow, curvy, with small towns spaced fairly evenly apart. I picked up my pace. Gray asphalt led me into the foothills. Lime-green digger pines became interspersed with the oak trees. As elevation rose, pines became the norm. At the outskirts of each town was a self-storage complex, about as long as a city block. Each had the same red and white walls and signage: AA *Self Storage.* I wondered: Does any population on earth have as much extra stuff as we Americans?

Bell kept to the speed limit. I advanced closer, falling behind a wide, white Dodge Ram 2500, a tank of a pickup truck that completely blocked view of my sedan from Hal Bell's rearview mirror. At reaching Highway 88, Bell turned left, east by northeast. I was in luck; the big pickup did the same. We climbed in elevation. Bell's route would take him—I thought—to one of his mining claims. He surprised me by turning onto Red Corral Road. Clyde Whitney's driver's license listed his address as 8124 Red Corral Road.

Was he fetching something for Clyde? Was he going there without Clyde's knowledge?

Bell pulled over, left, in front of a steel gate. The white pickup kept going. So did I. Spotting an opening on the right side of the road, I turned onto a flat outdoor parking area in front of a carport attached to a knotty-pine cabin. No vehicles were about. Either this was a vacation home, or the owners were away. If someone showed up, I was practiced at pretending to be lost.

I walked across the road and picked my way uphill through manzanita trees with spear-like branches peeling thin flakes of ruddy bark, and lanky pine trees. The day's heat increased. Binoculars around my neck, I carried the notebook and camera. My phone wasn't good enough for long shots. The notebook, rather than using my phone, was a holdover from my Clint Sherman old-days style of doing business.

Clyde Whitney's house was two stories, with three upstairs

dormer windows. The front few feet of Bell's pickup were visible to the left of the house, which I viewed from behind. I recorded time and date in the notebook. Thirty minutes later, Bell emerged from the back door and stepped onto a deck stained a dull red. I zoomed the camera and shot photos. Under the mushroom-colored cowboy hat, Bell's face and neck had the appearance of a man who lived more outdoors than indoors. His eyes were brown, his nose upturned as if perpetually sniffing for something.

Bell checked to be sure the back door was locked, re-hid a key under the porch, then went around the side of the house. His Toyota pickup, as worn as his skin, backed around. Bell drove off. I hustled to the paved road and ran across it to the sedan, started the car and watched my phone. Bell headed down curvy Red Corral Road toward the Mokelumne River. Shortly before reaching it, he turned left onto a space unmarked on the phone's map, and stopped. A minute later he proceeded, indicating he'd likely opened a gate and let himself onto private land. I continued down Red Corral Road, following power poles. The last one was near a tall steel gate topped with barbed wire, presumably the entrance to Watters Mine. I crossed the river and started up the other side of the canyon. I pulled over where I could, hoping to get a look at the mine and perhaps Bell through binoculars. Other than more of the fence topped with barbed wire, I saw only trees and rocks.

I walked to stretch the legs, and to find a spot where I saw buildings or movement, finally descending to the river. Gazing upward, I saw nothing more than before. Below me, in green river pools, baby trout wriggled against the current. I went back to the car and ran the engine with the windows shut and the air conditioning at full blast.

Hours passed slowly. I hadn't remembered to bring a book. Then darkness came quickly, as it does in canyons. Finally, Bell left. I gave him a half mile lead. His route suggested he was returning to the Sacramento area. Bell drove slowly. I drove slowly. Cars stacked up behind me. It was too dark to see a place to safely pull over and let people pass. So when my phone indicated Bell turned left onto Highway 16, I turned left onto Lone Pine Road, which rounded its way past ranches all the way to near Sacramento. I needn't worry Bell would pick up on being tailed. I daydreamed about Karen Brady.

Headlights raced up from behind. I looked down and saw I was going twenty-five, too slow for a wide country road, even at night. I picked up speed. The high beams of the vehicle behind me clicked on. I thought: a local rancher having fun. The SUV or truck came up too close for comfort, as if it might ram the back of the sedan. I kept my eyes on the road to avoid the glare I'd get by looking into the rearview mirror.

I went into an elongated, broad right bend. The vehicle behind me roared out to the left. Its engine screamed. I slowed, to let it pass. It swerved at me. I reacted, swerving right and pressing the brake. A flickering glance left: a large white pickup. It swerved at me again. Its horn blared. I tried for a look at the driver. The truck swerved at me yet again. Forced to pull to the right, I skidded over dirt into the trunk of an oak tree. The white truck's lights snapped off. I couldn't make out the license plate. The pickup disappeared around the bend.

I scrambled out of the sedan. Dust drifted in headlights. The dust smelled dry, a smell that mixed with the smell of burned rubber and that of a heated engine. The right rear of the sedan had a dent the size of a garbage can lid. I shouted profanities at the empty road. Walking back around the sedan, to get in and drive off, an engine roared and high beams raced around the broad curve at me like a locomotive.

Brakes slammed. The driver's door flung open and stayed open as a man hopped down from the elevated truck. I'm tall, a hundred and ninety pounds. Every other morning, I run a couple of miles. The days between I lift weights. While employed by Clint Sherman, at times things got physical. I'd enjoyed it.

Of average height, not of average build, the man had thick arms and a barrel chest. He stopped five feet in front of me. The glare of headlights deprived me of a look at his face.

I put up my fists. I spoke over the big pickup's grinding engine. "Why are you following me?"

He said, "You were following *me*. You stayed on my ass for the better part of an hour."

"It's one lane each way." I stepped sideways, away from the sedan, to give me more room. "We were going the same direction."

"I found that out."

Balanced on the balls of his feet, the man's eyes angled downward, as if he were looking at my knees. He took a step forward.

I said, "Back off."

I jabbed him twice, with lefts, using my superior reach to catch his cheek and smack him backwards. Another jab was followed by a hard slap with my half a right hand. I figured it wouldn't be long and I'd have him speaking in a different tone of voice.

He charged. We tied up, with my right arm wrapped around his neck. I'd learned to use my right hand like a hook, twisting an opponent's neck before forcing him to the ground. I cranked it, so he'd buckle when I punched him in the stomach. I swung my left fist; he turned into me hard and flipped me over his shoulder—*thud*, I tasted dirt.

I rolled away, got to my feet. We circled around, darting forward and back. Woozy from striking the ground, I took in a gulp of air.

I said, "Why were you following me?"

He dove for my legs. Take down. Keeping my left arm pinned behind my back, he punched me in the kidneys. It knocked the wind out of me. My exhale sounded like the wheezing of a man shot. He hopped up and before I could try another roll-away he stomped me several times, kidneys again. He walked away. The driver's door to the big pickup truck was still open. He hopped in without glancing in my direction.

The truck roared by, spraying dust over me.

I spun on the ground but couldn't catch the license plate.

I'd lost a few fights over the years, but none as lightning quick as that. I remembered something one of the guys at Sherman Investigations told me early on: "Never box a good wrestler. Your only hope is to go for the balls."

Five

By the time I returned the Sherman Investigations sedan to its rented parking space, and drove home, it was midnight. Since lurching into the tree, I'd been considering what to tell Karen. I played it safe, texting, *Nothing much with Bell. Looking forward to tomorrow.*

We made lunch together at her place. I was damn sore but didn't mention it. I reviewed tailing Hal Bell. That Bell had access to her grandfather's house key. That he spent five hours at the off-limits gold mine made me interested in Karen's fears about people going after her grandfather's rumored riches. Being run down by the white whale of a pickup truck multiplied suspicions that something nefarious was going on.

I said, "By the way, first time I was here, Bell and the housekeeper were arguing. They were around the corner from the front door. I couldn't make out their words, but they weren't singing Kumbaya."

Karen said, "He was probably telling Katia to look after Grandpa better. They've gotten into it over her forgetting about him in the back guesthouse."

"Maybe," I said. "Maybe not. They shut up fast when they saw me. Then Bell walks away without asking what I'm doing here. Like he was caught at something. It was strange."

We finished a couple of buffalo burgers with sautéed veggies, and spooned on the couch. I was discovering the wonderful knolls and prairies of Karen's skin.

Her cell rang. She checked the name of the caller. "Mind if I answer?"

I played with the fingers of her hand not holding the phone. "Yes and no."

Karen tapped her phone, said hello, and listened. She reached back and pulled her ponytail around to her lips. She said, "Be right over," and clicked off.

"Be right over where?"

"Uncle Stan and Aunt Laura's. This is as good a time as any for you to meet them."

"I think I'll pass. Let them get used to seeing my car here a little more."

"Uncle Stan says somebody broke into Grandpa's house in Pine Grove, and trashed it."

"What?" On my feet, I said, "Does your grandfather have any other old buddies who might be looking to steal his gold? Bell wasn't in the house long enough to trash it. I just don't see him making a mess of things."

Karen took me by an arm. "Come on, let's see what's going on."

"Only if I get a raincheck on the couch."

Karen rolled her eyes. "Whatever, Taylor." We went outside, around the pool, passed the glass tables and entered the house through a back door.

Stan Whitney: same height as Karen, fifty years old, extremely energetic. Later I learned he'd played college baseball and hit a lot of home runs. His hair was blonde on top, paler at the temples. Clean shaven, his eyes were cerulean blue. In a powder-blue Polo shirt and tan slacks, he seemed to smile as easily as he breathed.

Laura Whitney was maybe ten years younger. Whitish-blonde

hair caressed the tops of her shoulders. Parted in the middle, it hung straight. Her eyes were so pale I couldn't detect a color. She sported a short white dress that could pass for a tennis outfit, no stockings. Two juicy diamond rings sparkled on her left hand, a diamond bracelet on her right wrist. She wore diamond earrings and an emerald necklace with diamonds running across its bottom arc. Laura Whitney sparkled like a hotel chandelier.

Introductions were made in their formal-feeling informal side breakfast nook, which held a table for ten and two shiny, life sized, white alabaster sculptures I took to represent a female and a male. Laura flinched at touching my hand. Stan saw this and avoided shaking hands by giving me a buddy slap on the shoulder. Karen claimed we'd met at the UC Medical Center, and slipped in I was in medical school. This seemed to sit well with her aunt and uncle.

Laura said, "We've been wondering about Karen's visitor. She's kind of private about these things."

Stan slapped my shoulder a second time. "Nonsense," he bellowed. "We just need to give her a little time. Don't forget, we haven't seen much of each other in years."

This came across as criticism.

Stan led us through the kitchen into a high-ceilinged great room. He walked with the slightly pigeon-toed bearing athletes who are capable of short bursts of speed often do. Sanded eucalyptus logs served as exposed beams. The furniture, paintings and sculptures were arranged in a way that in itself was a work of art. I took an offered armchair in front of a fireplace fronted by tiny brownish tiles. Bowled over by the room's grandiosity, I was too dazzled to notice Laura leave. She returned with a bottle of Samuel Adams beer in each hand. They went to Karen and me. Laura circled back for two more. Stan watched this performance with seeming admiration. Laura was back before I could catch up with my thoughts. Handing a beer bottle to Stan, she curtsied. I think this was supposed to be amusing. It wasn't.

We settled onto plush dark chairs. I waited for the bullshit to begin.

Stan said, "Jeff, I'm glad you're here. As a physician, you'll understand the situation we're facing with my father. He's suffering from late-stage dementia. Perhaps you have some advice."

"Let's be clear. I'm still a medical student." I caught Stan staring at my trashed hand. I felt like waving it, just to shake him up. "As to an opinion about your dad, Karen specializes in elders. My field is children."

This threw Stan off course. For about one second.

He said, "We're proud of Karen. She walks away from that tech company and goes into something charitable."

Laura displayed a bright happy face. "Absolutely. She's going to save lives."

Heat rose to my head. I swigged cold beer and resolved to keep any thoughts to myself.

Karen said, "What happened up at Grandpa's house?"

Stan described receiving a phone call from his father's nearest neighbor. Bob Williams, retired navy, checked on the place whenever Clyde was away. He'd told Stan that while out on his morning walk, going past the gate at Clyde's house he saw the lock had been snapped off. The front door was ajar. He checked the house. The contents of drawers, cabinets and otherwise were scattered all over the floor.

I said, "Did this neighbor see anything unusual? Cars, or someone walking by? It sounds like it's out in the country. Most anyone coming along might stick out."

Stan shook his head. "He says no. Nothing."

Karen said, "That's awful. I'll go straighten things up. See what needs fixing."

Stan said, "I don't think that's necessary."

Laura squealed a dismissive giggle. "Duh. Karen's not a *housekeeper*. Besides, she's got school."

Karen said, "Really. I'm happy to help."

Laura said, "That's sweet of you." She turned to Stan. She crossed her bare legs toward him. She made a casual flip of her gaudy rings. "Honey, have a couple of your people go in the morning. Let them do any fixing that's needed."

Stan took a sip of beer. He wiped his lips with thick fingers. "You're right." His words sailed with a tone of finality. "I'll go up with a couple workers in the morning. I'll bring a carpenter for any repairs."

Karen said, "I could meet you there."

Stan said, "I'll take care of this myself."

The huge room was cool, and as in Karen's place, I didn't see an air conditioner. The fireplace did not exude any wood smoke smells. Other than the beer in my hand, the room seemed magically without scent. I realized that the artful arrangement of objects was, like Stan and Laura, a kind of performance. Karen was wise not to trust them.

To Karen, I said, "If it's basically cleaning up and organizing things… No offense, but it might turn out to be a case of too many cooks."

Karen fired me an in-control but rebuking look.

Stan's face signaled victory. "Thanks for being an impartial observer."

Laura swung her white-blonde hair. Diamonds twinkled. "Absolutely."

Two more minutes of nonsense talk about me being in medical

school and contributing to the betterment of humankind, and Karen sacrificing a lucrative career in high tech with a company that hawked a phone app that kept people apprised of activity on their phone apps, and we went out through the back door. We walked alongside the translucent blue water of the swimming pool. Its sweeper emitted a dull humming sound.

Karen said, "What's with the too many cooks bit? I wanted to kick you."

"If Stan's going up tomorrow, that gives us today to get there first. I always keep a dress shirt and tie in the car. If you change into something you'd wear to a museum, we can stop on the way out. I'll say it was nice to meet them. You say we're going to the Armin Hansen seascapes exhibit at the Crocker, downtown."

Karen said, "I'll drive."

"I'll get gloves from my car."

Six

[handwritten annotation: REGULAR LSD tripper a sign of acid trips — Those flecks]

Karen's dusky orange, four-door Volvo headed through oak trees and grasslands at a different angle from Crystal Meadows than I'd driven from Sacramento the day before. I tried not to look at Karen too often. It wasn't easy. Her eyes had amazing orange flecks around the green irises. They radiated good health. And Karen conducted herself with an elegance that knocked me into an exhilarating spell. My plan for a slow summer had evaporated in a most welcome manner.

Karen said, "What do you think of my aunt and uncle?"

"Your uncle reminds me of a man who tries to sell snow to Eskimos."

[handwritten annotation: AFTER 10 MINS. LACKING or pretty too HARSH]

"Aunt Laura?"

"On a trust scale of zero to ten, I give her a zero." *[handwritten annotation: 2 1/2]*

"We're on the same page."

We approached the Sloughhouse district. Orderly vineyards lined both sides of two-lane Highway 16. Rows of green leaves zipped by. Rustic enough to seem you were in another world from car stuffed, bustling Sacramento, the area was only thirty minutes from downtown. Two hip roadhouses served hearty food, craft beers, local zinfandels and cabernets. Both of their parking lots were filled.

[handwritten annotation: not the AREA WINES PINOTS CHARDS]

Checking my phone, I saw that Hal Bell was home, as he'd been all day.

34

After turning onto Highway 49, we drove through towns with main streets of brick buildings and old wooden ones. Tall facades announced business names. Rolling along, the white pickup truck came to mind. Not telling Karen about it weighed on me. Thinking I didn't want to frighten her was disrespectful. A week into the relationship and I was already screwing up.

At Clyde Whitney's house, we parked in front of the gate. Pulled shut, with the snapped locked set back in place, it appeared as if nothing had transpired there. My tie long tossed onto the back seat, I rolled up the sleeves of my white shirt as we approached the front door. We donned blue surgical gloves. Karen, in a sleeveless purple cotton dress and sandals, tucked her chestnut ponytail into the back of her dress. We went around to behind the house. I took the key from under the deck, unlocked the back door and returned the key.

The first floor was covered with stuff pulled from drawers and cupboards. Seat cushions were strewn about. We turned on lights and pulled open yellow curtains. The house smelled of stale air. It looked to be circa the 1950s or 1960s, with knotty-pine paneling rather than sheetrock for walls.

I followed Karen upstairs. Three bedrooms. The floor of the one Clyde Whitney slept in was a mess, like downstairs, and like downstairs we found nothing important. The other two bedrooms were home offices. One contained gold mining materials, everything from pamphlets to books to maps. Everything was in order. The third bedroom was filled with rows of materials involving satellite technology. It too seemed untouched. A thief considerate regarding Clyde's life's work?

Karen and I returned to the first floor. A man stood with a pistol leveled at us in his right hand. On his upper arm a tattoo of a scorpion curled to under the sleeve of his dark T-shirt. Wearing a

AWKWARD

SCOTT LIPANOVICH

red baseball cap, the man was another guy whose face looked like it had endured a lot of weather. They just kept turning up. This one wore denim overalls. He had a shaggy brown mustache and a protruding belly. The nose was a rosy drinker's nose. His eyes moved from Karen to me, and back.

We raised our hands.

His words came gruffly, in a Southern drawl. "What the hell you-all doing out here?"

I said, "I hope you're Bob Williams."

The man had entered through the back door and left it open. He stood in a shaft of greenish light.

Karen said, "Are you the person who called my uncle about this?" She pointed to the mess on the floor.

The man looked Karen up and down. His body relaxed. He said, "I'll be hornswoggled. You're kin to Clyde." A smile came that didn't spread light, but it didn't threaten, either. "You got that clean living Mormon look, like Clyde does. I ain't saying you're Mormon. I'm just saying you look like kin of Clyde."

Hands still up, Karen said, "I'm Clyde Whitney's granddaughter. You called my uncle Stan about what happened here."

The pistol disappeared into the front bib of the overalls. "Okay, I'm buying." He wagged a finger. "But who's this?"

Karen said, "This is my boyfriend, Jeff Taylor. You *are* Bob Williams, right?"

"For fifty-seven years."

Our hands dropped. The whole house seemed to cool off.

Bob said, "What say we go over to my place and have us a confab?"

He turned off the lights. Karen and I pulled the yellow drapes closed. Bob motioned for us to go first. We walked out the back door. Bob locked it behind him without a glance. I wondered if he had locked that door before.

Karen and I dropped the surgical gloves on the floor in the back of her Volvo, crossed the street and went downhill to the pine cabin I'd parked in front of on Saturday. We sat at a round metal table painted white, under a white-fringed green umbrella planted down its center. Bob Williams cranked it so shade covered the three of us. Darlene Williams, about Bob's age, came outside, introduced herself and went back inside. She did not speak with a southern accent. Bob followed her. He returned with a pitcher of water. Ice cubes clinked as he set it down. Bob excused himself, went in the house and came outside with three opaque plastic glasses. The scent of pine trees floated in the breeze.

Bob launched into his autobiography. Born and reared in Houston, he'd wandered after high school, got into trouble, a DUI, drag racing on a state highway, and a non-injury hit and run. There had been pot in the car when he was arrested for the hit and run. The judge gave him a choice: five years in jail, mostly for the four ounces of pot, which the district attorney rightly said Bob was pedaling, or joining the military for an equivalent five years. Bob chose a hitch in the navy that turned into a career of thirty years. He met Darlene while stationed in Oceanside, up the coast from San Diego.

"When I got out, we bought this. A cash deal for everything we had. I was done with the ocean, done with cities." Bob brushed fingers across his thick mustache. "We planned on working part time, but between my pension, and Darlene's for putting up with smart-mouthed kids as a classroom aid for twenty-one years, we get by okay."

Karen and I sipped water, and listened. Bob seemed to feel a need to explain what navy life is like to civilians. He glanced at my bad hand a couple of times but didn't ask about it. Exactly one car passed during the time he delivered the story of his life.

I looked to the front yard ringed by Ponderosa pines. "You've made a good life here. Congrats."

Bob said. "Lucky for me, the judge nudged me into the service. Without that, there's no telling what trouble I would've found."

I said, "Can you tell us more about what happened at Clyde's? Karen's uncle says you were taking a walk, saw the lock to the gate was snapped, and the front door cracked open." *a SHIT ?*

"That's right. I take my morning constitutional at about nine. That's how I met Clyde. I'm out walking when he pulls up to the gate. I say 'howdy' and introduce myself." Bob looked to Karen, shook his head. A look of bemusement crossed his face. "Never met anyone like your grandpa. That first time, I thought he was half angel, half ghost."

Karen said, "How long ago was that?"

"Six-seven years. That man is a trip. It's not like we're close buds, but we get along. I keep a look on the place when I notice he's been away awhile."

Karen said, "Thank you."

Bob said, "I should also tell you, your Uncle Stan came by once and asked how I thought his daddy was doing. He slipped me a hundred, gave me his business card and asked me to call if I ever thought I should." Bob drank cold water, looked off as if recalling the conversation. "Your uncle seemed concerned about Clyde's welfare, wanting to know if he had any visitors and such."

I said, "What might 'such' be?"

"If Clyde seemed to be hauling up things from the mine. About the visitors, he fretted over Clyde being alone so much. I don't think being alone bothers him a single bit."

Karen said, "Before I forget, let me give you my cell number."

Bob removed a pair of glasses with thick black frames from his overalls. He perched them on his chunky nose. Then he pulled a phone from that ample front pouch. He squinted and tapped Karen's number into it. "Karen with a K?"

"For thirty-one years."

Bob snorted. "That's pretty good. Let me give you mine, in case something comes up and you need to reach me. Any time I can help Clyde, I'm there."

Karen entered Bob's number in her phone. She said, "I don't quite know how to put this. See, Uncle Stan and I are kind of territorial about Grandpa." Karen pulled that lovely chestnut-colored ponytail from the beneath the back of her dress, gave it air. She said, "He'd think I'm crossing a line by coming here without him."

Bob adjusted the glasses by lifting them with a thumb. He looked at Karen, then at me. "Go on."

Karen said, "If you could keep this conversation just between us, I'd appreciate it. Grandpa's health isn't the steadiest. There's no use stirring up bad blood in the family. We're all living at the same place now. Does that make sense?"

The glasses came off. Bob snapped them closed. They disappeared into the overalls with the phone and pistol. "You're good people. I see that."

Without speaking, I extracted three twenties and a five from my wallet, all the money I had, and set the green bills under my water glass. Karen and I stood. We shook hands with Bob Williams. When shaking mine, he looked me in the eye.

Karen promised we'd come back and visit sometime.

Seven

We wound our way back toward Pine Grove. At reaching the state highway, rather than turn toward Sacramento we went right and climbed into thicker, darker forest. We pulled over. Karen tapped Clyde's home address into her navigator. It gave us two possible routes. One took us past the Williams' house, where we could easily be seen. The other didn't. We journeyed down again, to the Mokelumne River. We crossed it and hooked up with Red Corral Road and followed the river downstream to a spot with enough room for Karen to park safely. From there we walked to the gate at Watters Mine. Again I saw green pools with trout waving tails to hold steady against the current.

As assumed, the gate was locked. It required a code. Karen tried Clyde's birthday, her grandmother's birthday, and 07/20/69, the day Armstrong walked on the moon.

Karen said, "Grandpa was the youngest person in the room, in Houston. He monitored the weather up there. He was proud to be part of history."

To each side of the gate ran cyclone fencing topped with lines of barbed wire. The barbed wire angled outward and up, making the fence impossible to climb. It went uphill into trees beyond where we could see, and downhill toward the river. We went that way, then scrambled over granite boulders and riverside land as the fence paralleled the Mokelumne River. In places where water splashed over rocks, its coolness reached us.

Half an hour later, the barbed-wire fence took a ninety degree turn to the left. We headed uphill, into pine forest.

I said, "How many acres is the mine property?"

Karen said, "I think it's a hundred and sixty."

"A hundred and sixty? We could be following this fence all afternoon."

Karen touched the long beak of her straw sun hat, reminding me of a Quaker. She stopped walking. "What do you think we should do?" She looked at me with those astonishing, orange-flecked green eyes. "You want to come all the way out here and give up? Just quit?"

We resumed walking along the fence.

I said, "Your grandfather must be one paranoid man to go to such lengths. One rich and paranoid man. I bet he spent more on this fence than the value of any gold he scared up."

Karen said, "Taylor, you're getting testy."

"That's right. I'm not good about rich people spending money on things like ludicrous fences, when there are lots of people who don't have enough to eat."

"You've made your point."

We climbed. The forest became dense. The cyclone fencing ended and was replaced by five lines of barbed wire strung between posts. Between the posts were sandwich-board no trespassing signs covered with years of dust and pine needle detritus. Below the admonition not to advance were outlines of a dog baring teeth and the warning:

Canine Patrolled

Go Back

Karen said, "That's funny. There weren't any dogs. My grandfather wouldn't hurt a flea."

41

We tore our clothes getting over the fence. We wandered through trees and rocks toward where we guessed the road coming in from the gate might be.

I said, "You've never been to the mine, right?"

"No way."

Ahead was a dirt trail. Karen said, "Nobody but Hal Bell and a couple workers when Grandpa first bought it. If anybody tries to get him to talk about the mine, he goes like this." Karen ran a finger across her lips, like the closing of a zipper.

Our feet made munching sounds on dried earth and pebbles. Through trees we saw the remnants of a gravel road. Weeds poked through. We followed it. A large tin building came into view, flat roofed and square, and smaller buildings of sun-bleached wood.

Once out of the trees, I used a hand to block sun glare. Karen broke into a run causing her Quaker hat to fly up behind her, and sink slowly, like a balloon settling to earth.

"Taylor!"

I ran after her, making out a stick-like figure in the shadow of a wood structure. Looking our direction, his eyes shone like flashlights. Clyde Whitney's white T-shirt was powdered with dust. He thrust clenched fists toward the sky.

Clyde shouted, "I am ready! I am ready to go home."

Karen shouted, "Grandpa!"

Clyde looked up, stretched harder for the sky. He lost his balance. He wheeled around. His work boots stirred up dust. Clyde stumbled, slowed, caught himself. He wheeled around again and fell to the ground seconds before we reached him.

Karen and I turned him over, getting his face out of the dirt. Clyde seemed not to be cognizant of our presence.

Karen said, "Grandpa, are you okay? Tell me if you're okay."

She stroked his white hair. I looked around for whoever was

there with Clyde. I knew it wasn't Hal Bell, because if he'd left his house my phone would have alerted me.

Clyde said, "I made an offering. To my maker."

Clyde opened his left hand. It held a Ziploc baggy of gold dust. He opened his right hand. The same.

I searched for movement in the buildings. I saw a dirt road that went uphill between trees.

Clyde's eyes fluttered. He gave me the Whitney frown. "Are you here to help me go?"

Clyde did not have an inkling of who I was. I said, "I'm here to be your friend."

Karen continued to stroke his white hair. She gently smoothed dirt off a cheek.

"Mr. Whitney," I said, "who did you come here with?"

Clyde said, "The safe is not safe."

I said, "That's right. But how did you get here?"

Clyde looked across the road to the large tin building. He squinched his eyes in an attempt at concentration. "Is this a test? To see if I'm ready?"

Karen and I exchanged somber glances.

Clyde turned onto his side. He reached into a back pocket and pulled out another small, half-filled baggy of gold dust. "I brought offerings. I am ready."

I drove us back to Crystal Meadows. Karen and Clyde sat in back. Whenever I could, I used the rearview mirror to observe the eccentric gold devotee. He seemed to hold no sense of where he had been or where we were going. I saw him turn to Karen. He smiled feebly.

"Caroline, it's kind of you to come all this way to see me. I appreciate it."

Karen said, "Caroline is your daughter, Grandpa. I'm Karen, your granddaughter."

Clyde said, "When did you get here?"

And so it went. One minute Clyde talked gibberish. In the next he recounted a childhood vacation to the Finger Lakes, in upstate New York, down to the color of a rowboat, pine cones lining the fireplace mantel, and raccoons that clattered on the back porch at night. He described an afternoon where the young cousins, jammed in the loft of the same rented cabin, dropped water balloons onto the adults who pretended to be sitting ducks in Adirondack chairs looking out on the lake. After this, Clyde's head sagged to where the back seat reached the right door. He fell into a peaceful sleep. It was sweet, and sad. Karen and I spoke little.

In Crystal Meadows, Karen woke him. We both walked him to his guesthouse. Karen went inside, to put Clyde to bed. She gave me the key to her place.

Taped to the door at Karen's guesthouse, a typed note:

Hi Karen,

We were under the impression you would only be away a few hours. We promised Roberta and Brad Blevins we'd make their anniversary BBQ, so we have to get going.

Clyde is at Hal Bell's, via Uber. He's taken it before. Hal's number is 916-483-7691. He'll probably drive Clyde home, but if not, Clyde has enough money for a return trip. Uber is so handy!

Laura

I dropped the note on the coffee table, went to the refrigerator for iced tea. I sat on the couch near the unused fireplace. I wondered what it was like being Clyde. Did it scare him when he realized he didn't know where he was? I hoped not. If anyone deserved to live without fear, it was soulful Clyde Whitney.

Karen entered the guesthouse. She carried the three Ziploc baggies of gold dust in her right hand. She set them on the oak coffee table. I pointed to the note. Karen read the note without picking it up.

She said, "There was a message on the guesthouse land line from Hal Bell. He checked in to see why Grandpa didn't get dropped off at his place. I called him back. I told him Grandpa had forgotten he was going." A rarity, Karen seemed anxious. "Stan and Laura don't even bother to call Bell to make sure Grandpa gets there okay?"

"That's lazy as hell."

Karen frowned. She shook her head. Her ponytail echoed this. Karen picked up the glass of iced tea, downed a swallow. "This shows you how little they really care."

I said, "So Stan or Laura put him in an Uber. But Clyde gives the driver directions to the mine? Maybe hands him money, so the driver takes him seriously?"

Karen stared at the note. "I'm sure he had it written down. When his mind's clear, he writes things like addresses on pieces of paper. Or like with the gate code. He usually doesn't remember to look for them. Today, I guess he did."

"What are you going to say to your aunt and uncle?"

"Nothing. They'd use this as an excuse to put him away somewhere. They've wanted to for months. My staying here is the only thing delaying it."

I heated leftover eggplant casserole in the microwave. Karen and I were tired from the long day, and saddened by Clyde's condition.

As I was about to leave, Karen handed me the three baggies of gold dust. "Could you take these for safekeeping? He won't remember them. I don't want them around for Hal or Katia to steal."

Karen went to the kitchen. She returned with a small brown paper sandwich bag. She slipped in the Ziploc baggies, kissed me on the cheek and pointed to the door.

Eight

That morning I'd called Clint Sherman and told him what happened with the sedan. His response was the usual for Clint: we were to meet at eight p.m., dinner at Frank Fat's. During the early years of Clint's career, Frank Fat's was the center of eating and drinking for Sacramento's high rolling lobbyists and politicians. One block from the Sherman Investigations office, three from the Capitol, Clint was on a first-name basis with the staff. His bills were tallied and mailed monthly. Clint paid with a check. A Scotch-on-the-rocks man, he winced at seeing me raise a bottle of Sierra Nevada Pale Ale.

The usual routine was plenty of talk before ordering meat. Once the food arrived, no more conversation.

I told Clint about Clyde Whitney and his attempt to glean gold from the runoff of the old mines.

Clint said, "I see the attraction. Take something everybody else thinks is played out, squeeze another round out of it."

I filled him in on the activities of the day before.

Clint said, "You were behind a vehicle that was behind your target for forty-five minutes. You didn't record the license number?" He tilted his head back. The low light of the restaurant made ochre reflections on his trifocals. "Are you kidding?"

"It didn't occur to me. One lane each way, curvy road, it's normal to be behind the same vehicle for long stretches."

Clint took a sip of Scotch, examined the glass. "At least nobody got hurt."

"I have no idea how he ended up behind me. Maybe he was parked farther up the river canyon when I was keeping tabs on Bell. If he saw me parked there for hours, he'd know I was watching Bell. But why go after me? Why not just tail, try to figure out who I am?"

I set down my beer. Clint eyed it with humored distaste.

I said, "Let me know about the damages. I don't want your insurance to go up because of me."

Clint took a measured, civilized sip. "Cut it out. When you become a rich doctor, I expect you to make good. Do we understand each other?"

I'd witnessed Clint say *Do we understand each other* to genuinely rough characters, looking them in the eye until they either looked away or nodded in surrender. It meant the subject was closed.

"Besides," Clint said, "this is getting interesting. Take another car and bang it up, for all I care. Just don't wreck things with the young lady. Every time you mention her, your face lights up like a Christmas tree."

The waiter approached. Clint lifted his right hand and made a circle with his forefinger, telling the waiter to take a few laps before returning for our order. "One more thing," he said. "I'm not suggesting it. It's a condition for you having use of Sherman Investigations resources. There's potentially big money involved in this. Untraceable money. Whenever there's a lot of untraceable money floating around, things tend to get hazardous. You're to check out a thirty-eight from the office."

I began to protest. Clint spoke over me. "No discussion, no excuses. I'll have Natalie do the paperwork."

The mayor and his wife, he in a tux, she in a long, cream-colored gown, came over to say hello to Clint. A trim, polished couple in their sixties, they were the kind of pair who still looked elegant on dance floors. They'd been to a fundraiser for inner-city kids and were unwinding at a place no one would bother them. Clint introduced me as Sacramento State's only All-America basketball player.

I said, "He's being too generous. It was honorable mention."

Clint said, "You should have made first team."

Mayor Shelley stepped behind his wife to touch the tops of my shoulders. "I saw you play. You were the real thing." The mayor took his wife by the hand. They went to a table mostly hidden by a five-feet-high partition.

Wednesday at the medical center, waiting for Dr. Fisher to return from lunch, I sat in his office reading up on cases of measles in infants. Soft knocking at the open door brought my eyes up. Hal Bell. Freshly shaved, he wore a clean, button down beige shirt. His right hand held a dark nylon bag with a slip knot at the top.

Bell was all smiles. "Hello, Jeff. How goes it?"

I clicked the computer screen closed. "You here for Mr. Whitney's treatment?"

"He's getting zapped as we speak."

"Come on in. Have a seat."

Bell stepped into the room. He looked behind him. "Is it okay to shut the door?"

"Not a problem."

Bell closed the door. He took the chair Clyde had sat in. "There's no privacy anymore. Not with the internet."

I swiveled the office computer screen away, clearing the view between us. I waited for Bell to continue.

He said, "It's no secret you've been seeing Clyde's granddaughter. Your car is around the house. So I, well, I looked into you."

"That sounds pretty boring."

49

"Bullpucky. You were a hell of a basketball player. I found articles about you all the way back to high school." Bell took a breath. He seemed nervous. His cleaned-up look didn't fit with the rough-hewn face and gravelly voice. "You were headed from Sac State to med school when, you know, the hand. Three years later, you turn up in the Town Talk column. It says you're working for the fanciest detective agency in town. Trying to find out if someone murdered that boy Watkins, the senator, hit with his car. You cracked the case. It was all over the papers."

"That seems like a long time ago." It didn't. Other than after my hand was sliced, those few weeks were the most intense of my life.

Bell lifted the tan bag, then set it on his thigh. He said, "I'd like to hire you. For some detective work."

Playing it as cool as I could, I said, "That stuff was a long time ago."

Bell leaned forward, "Medical school must be expensive."

"And all consuming. No thanks."

"What if I showed you something that whetted your appetite? Something that makes me think your girlfriend's grandpa's best buddy, me, might be in danger?"

He undid the slip knot, reached in the bag and pulled out the CarScout I'd clamped beneath the back bumper of his Toyota pickup.

Bell said, "You know what this is?"

"I don't."

"It's a friggin' tracking device. Pulled it out from under my back bumper. Didn't you used to be a detective?"

"The ones we used looked entirely different. May I?" I reached out my good hand.

Bell stepped forward and handed me the CarScout. I wanted to get hold of it, because if Bell moved, even for two seconds, faster than five miles per hour, my phone would ring, like it had when Bell headed out with Clyde to the medical center an hour before.

Bell said, "Saturday, I go to my claim. I have a mining claim up on Tiger Creek, near where it meets the Mokelumne. The whole way up, there's this white pickup behind me. Yesterday, I started thinking maybe it wasn't an accident. Something about the way the pickup never got closer, never got farther back."

I placed the CarScout on the desk. I pretended to check it out. "I don't know about that, but I think I can figure out how this works." I cancelled the call function.

Bell said, "I figure whoever was in the white pickup put it under my bumper."

"I can see why you'd think that."

Bell folded his arms across his chest. He seemed to be considering options. I pretended not to be interested.

Dr. Fisher came in. He left the door open. He wore a white lab coat; a ball-point pen poked out of its chest pocket. A somewhat short and soft-spoken man with watery eyes, he had a way of getting children to relax around him that I hoped to someday emulate.

I said, "Dr. Fisher, this is Hal Bell. He brings a friend in for radiation treatment once a week."

Bell said, "Good to meet you. Sorry, Jeff. I got to get back. If I'm not there when Clyde comes out, he'll get confused."

I looked to the CarScout on Dr. Fisher's desk. "I'll check this out for you." I fished my wallet from my slacks, and extracted a business card. "Can you call me at seven? By then I'll have had a chance to look this over."

Bell snatched the card. He moved fast for a husky man in his sixties. "Talk to you then."

Bell disappeared around the corner of the door frame.

Dr. Fisher looked through the open doorway. "What was that about?"

"I'm not exactly sure. He wants me to figure out how this works. Other than that, no clue."

Dr. Fisher stepped over, picked up the CarScout, turned it over in his hands. Eight inches long, it had two sets of steel clamps for attaching the device to the underside of a vehicle.

Dr. Fisher said, "What am I looking at?"

"It's a tracking device, used on cars."

"He brought it to you because?"

"I used to work for a detective agency."

"That's right. It was on your resume."

Dr. Fisher's focus was on helping sick kids get well and stay well. He never mentioned the incident again.

As soon as I was alone, I texted Karen. *Can you come by my house? I'll be there at five.*

Her reply: *I hope your intentions are not honorable.*

My reply: *Never.*

On the way home from the medical center, I stopped at Sherman Investigations. Natalie Thomas was the only person in. She'd been with Clint for decades. Natalie operated as a kind of air traffic controller for the various components of Sherman Investigations. Closely cropped black hair and clothes perpetually neat, her figure reflected vigorous morning swims. Waiting on her desk was the form you signed when employing company resources. I signed for a Smith & Wesson 38, and six bullets. Natalie attested to this with her signature. Taking the gun served as a way appease Clint, which was easier than trying to buck him.

I tucked the gun away under the driver's seat of my car. I'd gone three years working for Clint without firing a shot, and didn't plan on changing that.

Soon as I was home, I showered and changed. For her part, upon arrival at the brick bungalow Karen looked fresh as an alpine morning. For the first time since meeting her, the long thick chestnut hair was free of its ponytail. We kissed before she crossed the threshold. We kissed our way through the living room, stepping around a brown chair and the coffee table. As soon as we parted, before we'd get carried away, I told Karen about Bell's appearance at the medical center and his request to hire me, and that he was going to call at seven o'clock.

A smile bloomed. "What are you going to tell him?"

"I don't know. First things first."

Living room couches at my place and hers had become warm-up spots for love. Removing the nurse's uniform took finesse. It ended up wadded in a blue ball on the hardwood floor.

I stood from the couch, reached for her. Karen stood and I swooped her up in a swinging motion and started for the hallway. Her feet were higher than my head.

"Jeff! Don't! You're crazy."

"For twenty-eight years."

"Hey, you're stealing my line."

"You're stealing my heart."

Heading down the hallway, I turned sideways so Karen's feet wouldn't scrape the walls.

Karen said, "That's right. I'm going to steal your heart and take it with me everywhere."

In the bedroom, we loved each other so hard we required a shared shower to cool off before dinner. After dinner, snuggling on the couch, I thought: On behalf of Karen, who I'd known for two weeks, I'd followed someone with the goal of finding her grandfather's gold for her. Did Karen want that more than she wanted me? And what did I want? Everything with Karen was happening so fast, I hadn't given thought to that. I told myself to slow things down a little.

Waiting for Bell's call, I told Karen about nearly getting sideswiped, lurching off the road and skidding into an oak tree. Karen didn't interrupt with questions. She did frown. Once the frown emerged on her forehead, it stayed.

I said, "I didn't want to worry you. Now I realize it was disrespectful."

Karen's lips pursed. Her eyes wandered across the room. The frown pulled her eyebrows together.

Karen said, "I was married to someone who kept things from me. Some of it was financial, some was about another woman. He said he didn't want to worry me."

Karen's tone held none of the qualities of a sermon.

I said, "I've never cheated on anyone. Not once."

The frown lines let go. "I already told you I trust you. Now tell me what you're going to do with Hal Bell."

"Unless he proposes something bizarre, I think I'll take the job. I'm already trying to keep track of him. He's going to be on the lookout for tracking devices, so I may as well check up on him over the phone. Plus, I'll make some money."

Karen said, "Does this mean I have to start paying you, too?"

I heard Clint's voice in my response: "Cut it out."

My phone pinged five minutes early. I went to the brown armchair. My notebook and pen were in front of me, on the coffee table. I tapped my phone and said hello.

Hal Bell said, "You did a good job covering things when that doctor showed up. I was impressed."

I said, "Thanks." And nothing more. I've found that people with something to hide—like Bell's sneaking into Clyde's house and

Watters Mine—have little ability to let silence last. The less you talk, the more they talk.

The sound of Bell's breathing came through the phone. He seemed to hesitate before saying, "Can you make that tracking thing work?"

Inside the brick house it was always a little dark. Even so, Karen's green eyes danced with light. She wore white panties and one of my white T-shirts. I looked away from her to keep my mind on the task.

"Yes. And I erased the coding, so he—presuming it was a he—can't track it anymore. It will seem like the tracker died. Unfortunately, these things are designed so if they're discovered you can't trace back to wherever it sent the info." I made squiggles in the notebook. "What do you have in mind?"

The sound of throat clearing. "Is being a detective like attorney-client privilege? I mean, something I tell you, you can't blab to anyone else?"

"Yes and no. If you're working with a licensed detective, you have attorney-client privilege, with a couple of exceptions. One is if a judge issues a subpoena. Another is if the detective comes across a crime that needs to be reported to the police. General speaking, that means violence."

"Who said anything about violence?"

"I'm just answering your question. I'm no longer licensed, so you don't have those rights with me. I value discretion, but it's not like attorney-client privilege."

Bell said, "I hate lawyers."

Rather than comment, I gave him another dose of silence.

Then Bell said, "I need you to give me your word you won't tell the party involved. Won't tell the individual about it. Can you do that for me?"

"You'd get discretion."

A third dose of silence. I heard a faint buzzing in the phone. The thought crossed my mind that Bell could be taping our conversation. His lie about going to his mining claim rather than saying he went to Clyde Whitney's house and Watters Mine put me on guard. It added to the strangeness of bumping into him at the Whitney compound and Bell scooting along without mentioning the coincidence that we'd met in Dr. Fisher's office that afternoon.

Bell said, "I can't pay more than five hundred a week. But this would be very part time. Track him with that thing, and keep your eyes and ears open. Can you be good with that?"

"If I took the job, will it be hard to locate who it is you want me to tail?"

"Nope. I want you to bird dog Stan Whitney. Learn what he's up to as best you can. I figure a person with your background—an article about you said single mom, welfare—doesn't like that phony pretty boy anymore than I do. If you tell him about this conversation, I'll deny it. I'll say you're just out to stir up trouble within the Whitney family."

"Why would Stan Whitney have you followed?"

I looked over at Karen. Her eyes flared.

Bell said, "I can't think of anyone else who would. By things he's said, he's made it clear he thinks I'm after any gold Clyde has socked away."

"Are you?"

"Hell no. I worked with Clyde for years. I pretty much got him started at his first operation. He needed someone with construction experience. He paid me fair and square. He's like an uncle to me."

"Okay. I'll be in touch. If you see me in Crystal Meadows, we ignore each other."

Bell said, "I can do that."

We said goodbyes and clicked off.

Karen threw me one of her frowns. "You lied awfully easily. It's a little scary."

"You beat me to it when you called Bell and told him Clyde forgot about coming over that time."

Karen said, "Touché."

"I would've done the same thing."

I joined her on the couch. Karen's narrow frame was always warm. One by one, the joys of being intimate with a woman were returning. I loved the feel of Karen's skin on my fingertips. Every time we were intimate was like being lavished with a four-course meal.

I said, "Bell lied to me about going to your grandfather's. He said he went to his mining claim on Saturday. That gives me the right to lie back to him."

Karen took hold of my bad hand. "Do we know what we're getting into?"

"That's never stopped me before."

Nine

Someone was behind the actions of the driver of the white pickup. Stan Whitney was a logical suspect. I remembered how he'd been opposed to Karen going to Clyde's house and helping with the cleanup. Why?

Stan drove a silver Mercedes SUV. Rather than use the detached garage, which was a bit of a hike from the main house, he parked under a tile-roofed *porte cochere* attached to the right side of the house as you faced it. Always in a hurry, Stan entered and exited from there. For almost a week I couldn't get near the silver SUV without risk of getting caught. I told Bell he didn't need to pay anything until I planted the CarScout.

On Sunday, Karen was scheduled to bring supplies to Clyde Whitney's other mining friend, Rattlesnake Johnson, up the Sacramento River on Genoa Island. Karen explained he was blind; I remembered Clyde saying something about a blind rattlesnake. Now it made sense. Sort of. Karen and Bell were taking turns bringing Rattlesnake supplies, giving Hal Bell a break from so much Clyde Whitney duty. I wondered why Stan and or Laura didn't step up, then guessed that to help had never occurred to them.

The Sacramento River, broad, silty, drifted slowly past downtown. Once outside the city, the way to follow it upstream was to take Garden Highway, an elevated levee road. Air crooned through open windows. To our left flowed the silent brown river. Wild grape vines connected splendid oak and cottonwood trees. The vines hung like green-and-purple quilts.

Garden Highway crossed a slough near the confluence of the swifter Feather River and the lolling Sacramento. A careening swarm of blackbirds filled a chunk of sky as large as a football field. Karen had me pull off at a dirt road blocked by a steel bar painted white. She explained that the only way to get to Clyde's island was to cross private agricultural land to a bridge, and that buying the island included an easement. She twirled two thick combination locks, opened the gate, locked it after I drove through. We passed enormous rice paddies, harvested for the season, and drained. They dipped below road level, to our right. The flat plane owned an interesting russet color.

We stopped at a gate to a bridge spanning a canal that separated Genoa Island from the mainland. As at Watters Mine, cyclone fencing topped with barbed wire blocked anyone attempting entrance.

Karen recited a code for me to tap. The gate crept backwards on rubber wheels, accompanied by a deep, slow, groaning. Like cymbals concluding a piece of impassioned music, the heavy gate clanged at hitting a raised rail along the side of the steel bridge. A mucky smell rose from the canal's shallow water.

Twenty yards in was a stand-alone solar system, three shiny panels perched six feet above ground. No wires carrying electricity were in evidence. I figured the solar panels, sitting under sweltering Sacramento Valley sun, powered the fence. Shortly past them a dirt road peeled off to the left. A quarter mile later, one went to the right. A third road went right, disappearing in the shadows of valley oak trees and slim digger pines. We continued going straight. A woebegone rural outpost came into view: a wood cabin;

a large metal building with a generator outside and water pipes running to inside; a dust-coated tractor; three small structures that looked like storage sheds. A goat with tinkling bells around its neck stepped in our direction, turned its head and looked at the Jetta with one eye. To park I merely turned off the engine.

We climbed out.

A hunched, gray-bearded man at least seventy years old stepped from the wood cabin onto a low front porch. He ambled around a faded wood table and two faded wood chairs. With each step, his right leg bowed outward and swung back to center as his foot hit the deck boards. He wore a long-sleeved work shirt, and jeans. Both seemed slept in. He trotted down two stairs, onto dirt. Rattlesnake Johnson walked toward us without hesitation. His eyes were blank and milky. His tangled gray beard reminded me of a bird's nest. Behind him, a Winchester rifle rested against the cabin wall.

Rattlesnake said, "Who goes there?"

"It's me, Karen Brady. Clyde's granddaughter."

I said, "Hello, Rattlesnake."

"That's right. It's Sunday. But who's that with you?" His voice was parched, thin, high-pitched. "The tall one."

I looked to Karen. She gave me a non-committal shrug.

Karen said, "Jeff helped me get everything for today."

Rattlesnake Johnson extended his right hand. We walked to him. I took his right hand with my left.

Rattlesnake squeaked, "That's a strange handshake, mister."

"My right hand's half cut off. I didn't want to surprise you."

His grin was that of an old codger who'd had time to contemplate the world. "I can't remember the last time anything surprised me. You get past all that." Rattlesnake headed back to the two stairs and porch. "I was about to heat up my latest concoction. Come have some rabbit stew. Caught it in my own trap."

Karen and I unloaded the car. Rattlesnake carried the bags inside; Karen told me the cabin was a mess and he didn't want anyone to see it. On Rattlesnake's third pick-up round, a yellowish tabby cat scooted out the cabin's door, jumped onto a chair, then the table, purred and arched its back. I looked around. The outpost existed in a state of grubby semi-chaos. I thought about how vastly different this was from the tech, big-money world of satellites Clyde had spent most of his life amidst. It caused me to admire him even more.

The rabbit stew, fortified with turnips, carrots and what I feared was local grass, turned out to be tasty. Blue jays stopped by and squawked, resting on the porch railing.

Rattlesnake gazed blankly in my direction. "I started all this with Clyde. Until that greasy Hal Bell came aboard, from the other operation. Good worker. He knows his stuff, but I don't trust him."

I said, "Why?" *Why not?*

Rattlesnake chewed at his lower lip. "Clyde's a secretive creature. I got it right away. As long as the checks didn't bounce, I never asked questions. Just did as requested." Rattlesnake pointed toward the large metal building. "Bell, he's always trying to get Clyde to talk about what's going on inside Hotel Tin over there. Keeping Bell in the dark was a game to Clyde. He enjoyed it."

Karen leaned over, touched the sleeve of Rattlesnake's stained shirt. "You know Grandpa as well as anyone."

The wrinkles on Rattlesnake's tan forehead drew into a half circle. "Tell me, how is Clyde faring? Bell says he barely gets out anymore."

Karen said, "Between the cancer and dementia, he's—sorry to say this—he's really sinking."

A tear, then a second tear, rolled down Karen's cheek. I squeezed her hand.

Rattlesnake turned his blank eyes to me. "Clyde Whitney's my patron saint. After we got this place up and running, I went down to Mexico, to look into a silver mine. On the way back I fell asleep at the wheel. Cost me my sight."

Rattlesnake patted his knee. The yellow tabby, shooed off the table when stew arrived, hopped onto Rattlesnake's lap. He stroked it, which seemed to soothe both he and the purring cat. "So what does Clyde do? He says now I'm caretaker. In charge of security. He's made sure I'm fed ever since. God bless his pure soul."

Karen said, "When his mind's clear, he asks how you're doing."

"Tell him I'm fine. Tell him I ask about him, too."

"Of course," Karen said.

I got up and walked to the end of the porch. I rested my hands on the railing. It creaked.

Karen said, "Last time I was here, we talked about what will happen after Grandpa passes. Remember?"

I turned around. Rattlesnake stroked the purring tabby. He said, "Only too well."

Karen said, "When his mind goes completely, we might never find out if he has gold somewhere. Maybe a lot. As you know, my Uncle Stan is starting to work with the county on turning the island into a boating resort."

Rattlesnake nodded. I returned to the worn wood table.

Karen said, "If Hal Bell finds gold, you know he'll keep it. I think the same's true with Uncle Stan."

Rattlesnake guided the cat off his lap. He slid his empty white bowl aside, put his elbows on the table and set his cheeks on cupped palms. "Once Clyde passes, your uncle will throw me out on my keister." Right then he was a frightened man, not a sharp old timer.

Karen said, "If you help me find gold, it'll be shared fairly. My mom, my aunt, and Uncle Stan. No matter what happens with the island, my mom and I will make sure you have a roof over your head. We know that's what Grandpa wants."

Rattlesnake said, "What about this fellow? Can we trust him?"

"Definitely."

Rattlesnake Johnson pushed himself up from the table. He went to the cabin wall and lifted a saddlebag from a nail. "Clyde always brought food, and batteries for the radio. That's a hint. I'm low on batteries." Rattlesnake went to where the railing ended at the stairs and draped the saddlebag over it. "He'd fill this up, or part way up. With gold? I never asked. I couldn't see. He'd put this on Henry Ford and they'd tromp off. They'd be gone a good two-three hours."

At hearing its name, the goat clattered onto the porch. Its fur was small black coils. Rattlesnake's hands went out. The goat licked them, bringing chimes from the bells around its neck.

Rattlesnake said, "Maybe he'll lead you to pay dirt."

I wrapped the saddlebag around the goat's middle. It ambled off the porch. Henry Ford led us to a trail that wound through coyote bushes with digger pines and oak trees popping up here and there. A pair of rabbits bounded across the path like tiny deer. We moved at a slow jog. The path reached a dirt road. Henry Ford went left. He broke into a sprint and we ran like hell to not to lose sight of the fuzzy black goat. Another dirt road. Then a fork. Henry Ford stopped. He bleated, stepped off the road and tore off pieces of brittle coyote bush. Crunchy eating sounds joined the tinkling bells. We waited for where he would go next. A ways down the new road sat a stack of small broken concrete chunks, like a trail marker. I grabbed two, packed them in the saddlebag, got another two and evened the load.

I said, "Maybe the weight will trigger his memory," and gave Henry Ford a robust swat on the rump. He didn't move.

Karen said, "That's not the way."

She rubbed behind one of Henry Ford's ears. She brushed her cheek along the side of the goat's neck. Henry Ford's head bobbed up and down as if in encouragement. He finished chewing, turned half a circle, and walked straight into brush, bleating nonstop.

Karen grinned. "See? Love conquers all."

Henry Ford proceeded methodically. Remnants of a path appeared; Henry Ford took it. We followed. Quail made high pitched chugging sounds and skittered out of the way. About ten minutes later, we reached a four-inch in diameter white PVC water pipe. Henry Ford trotted next to it; we followed. The plastic pipe led us back to the wood cabin and outbuildings. I removed the small chunks of concrete from the saddlebag, tossed them into brush. I returned the saddlebag to the nail, which was a couple of feet over from the leaning rifle.

Rattlesnake Johnson came outside. He picked what looked like a bit of rabbit stew from his beard. His parched voice squeaked, "We rich yet?"

After the excursion with the goat, Karen and I said goodbye to Rattlesnake. She promised to tell Bell to bring batteries next time. In the Jetta, we explored a few of the dirt roads on Genoa Island. There were at least a dozen. The land gave off a lonely feeling, its vegetation sparse whenever we got near the Sacramento River. We came upon another fork where a stack of concrete chunks seemed a marker. We followed the weedy route until it dead-ended at a sizeable mound of what I assumed was silt Clyde had sifted through and then dumped with the tractor.

I said, "Your grandfather's theory is when silt was washed down river from hydraulic mining, it carried millions of bits of gold. I guess billions. From what I've read, the island almost doubled in size by the build-up of silt over decades. After it dried out for a hundred years, he decided to harvest it. It's brilliant."

Karen said, "We don't know how much he got. Just these little packets here and there."

The brown swathe of river ran north in pretty much a straight line for a hundred more miles up the Sacramento Valley. We didn't see all of the river until we reached it. We couldn't because the cliff-like bluffs of the island fronted the river forty feet above the water line. In some places the bluffs were reinforced by concrete, in others by tightly packed, tar-coated telephone poles. The steepness of the bluffs made it almost impossible to anchor and ascend them. And if someone did, like at Watters Mine, signs were placed picturing a dog with bared teeth and the warning:

Canine Patrolled

Go Back

I parked. We walked above the river.

"How in the hell is your uncle going to build a resort out of this? I mean, look around."

Karen said, "If he gets it through the county, he'll have a waterfront gas station and a general store. Who knows how many docks. The centerpiece will be a hotel, bar, restaurant and legal card games. The county always wants more sales tax."

I looked at the scrubby flat land. I remembered that Los Angeles used to be a desert. Shimmering modern cities along San Francisco Bay used to be soggy marshes. California's history is awash in money-making transformations that seemed preposterous at inception. I imagined Genoa Island dotted with flesh-colored stucco buildings. I imagined gurgling fountains with coins tossed in for good luck. I'd researched Stan Whitney. He was exactly the kind of real estate hustler to pull it off.

Walking, we found another mound of dried silt.

Karen said, "This was supposed to be Grandpa's last great accomplishment." She eyed the desolate land. "The truth is, his quote 'Heaven' is depressing."

I spun a hundred and eighty degrees. I headed straight for the car. I said, "Let's go."

Karen said, "Hey Taylor, what's the rush?"

I waved for her to catch up. "When Clyde wandered into the office that day, he said, 'The safe is not safe. But the ceiling at heaven is golden.' I thought it was some kind of spiritual metaphor. You know how he talks. Maybe it's literal. Maybe the mine's ceiling is filled with gold."

Karen said, "It could mean anything. He calls the whole island Heaven. He never calls it Genoa."

"The whole island doesn't have a ceiling."

Karen surprised me by saying, "Holy shit."

We explained the situation to Rattlesnake.

He looked blankly into a kind of blind person's middle distance. "I feel I don't got a choice." Rattlesnake gestured toward the Winchester rifle leaning against the cabin wall.

"I always thought I'd use that on anyone who tried to enter Clyde's operation. It's his church." Rattlesnake wagged his right arm overhead and pointed toward the expansive metal side of the largest building in the ramshackle enclave. "Clyde can't do nothin' with Hotel Tin now. So I got three choices: rely on Bell, your fancy-pants uncle, or you and this tall feller. I choose door number three."

He tugged at his whale-gray beard. "What the hell. Let me get you folks a key."

Rattlesnake went inside the cabin. I went to the car for flashlights.

The steel door rested on small hard rubber wheels, like the gate to the island. Karen unlocked the door. I pushed it open. It didn't give easily, sounding like chalk scraping a blackboard. Inside smelled of long-settled water in the concrete basins, and damp soil. Light from the opened door invaded the metal tomb about one third in. It was like entering a damp cave. The lights wouldn't work without getting the generator running. Neither of us knew how to operate it, or even if the generator still carried fuel. Unlike the run-down cabin and outbuildings, pipes, and untended machinery outside, the inside of Hotel Tin was an orderly, well-organized enterprise.

A vintage black safe, big as a refrigerator, squatted on a concrete pad. The zing of pumping adrenaline rang in my ears.

I shined the flashlight on it. Karen tried Clyde's birthday as the combination. It worked. I shined the flashlight across six shelves inside. Nothing. I checked for side compartments, perhaps half hidden. Nothing.

I said, "Let's try something."

I shut the heavy black steel door, turned the dial right, left, right, at random, pulled on the handle. The door opened. I shut the door, did the same thing. The door clacked open. I said, "Clyde's right. The safe is not safe."

Karen and I split up. What must have been a type of sluice box for separating specks of gold from traces of silt was to the right. It sat about chest high. Unlit banks of fluorescent lights ran the length of it. A water pipe led to the big trough, and out a tin side wall. There was no true ceiling, only a tin roof supported by a triangulated set of wood posts and roof rafters, probably Hal Bell's contribution.

Karen called, "I found one."

"Found what?" I shined my flashlight her way.

Karen waved a Ziploc baggy like a winning ticket. "It was on the ground, like it had been dropped by accident." She disappeared from my light. I heard her taking steps. "Here's another. Same size."

I scoured the ground, being careful not to trip on the water pipe.

"Bingo," I said. "The same baggie. Half full, like the rest. Maybe it's a certain weight in each one."

Karen said, "It seems so."

I searched the area around the water trough, and under the curve of the exiting pipe. "Bingo again."

We found eight baggies of gold dust. If each baggy held three ounces, each was worth roughly six thousand dollars.

Clyde Whitney had spent twenty years working that sluice box in whatever method he used before his mind disintegrated. It seemed reasonable to think a major stash resided somewhere.

Karen returned the key to Hotel Tin. She told Rattlesnake we'd found gold dust and emphasized it was important to keep that between the three of us.

Rattlesnake said, "I know what's best for me."

We exchanged a second round of goodbyes. Rattlesnake didn't wave because one hand petted the black goat while the other petted the yellow tabby.

In the car, Karen said, "This is going to your house, with the others. I don't want it anywhere near my place. Not with Uncle Stan and Hal Bell around."

Ten

On the drive back I didn't take in the majestic oak and cottonwood trees lining the great river, or the shimmering metal skiffs with fishing poles poking over their sides. I didn't sneak glances at the beautiful woman who arrived out of nowhere and in a couple of weeks had become central to my life. Instead, my mind unspooled images of Ziploc baggies half filled with gold dust. I wondered how many more we'd find. And maybe keep at my house. I didn't bring up the subject. Neither did Karen.

Even with some tuition waivers, by the time I finished medical school I'd be a hundred and eighty thousand dollars in debt. Of course I had zero claims regarding Clyde's gold. Then again, if Karen and I were together...

We talked about what might happen with Rattlesnake Johnson. Like Clyde, he was a free spirit and shouldn't be tucked away in a group home.

I said, "Does he have family?"

Karen said, "Yes. The Whitneys. Also an ex-wife who left him years ago because he spent all his time looking for gold. Genoa Island's his whole life now. If he's moved, he'd have to relearn everything. Where things are. How to walk from one room to another."

Was Karen avoiding talk about gold because she worried I'd want to keep some for myself? Or maybe she didn't want to appear greedy. On and on my thoughts spun. To our left rows of walnut trees flitted by. I was sure Karen didn't need money. When you grow up poor, you develop a keen sense of who is well off. It can be a snooty attitude, usually accompanied by conspicuous consumption. At the same time, growing up wealthy sometimes gives a person a certain ease that leads to being comfortable in one's own skin.

Like Karen Brady.

I'd never had a period of life when I was comfortable in my own skin. As a child I was insecure in my relationships with friends, not wanting them to see the small, disheveled, converted barn I lived in. I'd say my parents were divorced when in truth I'd never met my father and knew nothing about him. The loneliness of my early years, which during high school and college had ebbed, had come back with the isolation I self-imposed after those fingers were chopped off.

Twenty-eight years old, on my way to becoming an MD, involved in a relationship that held great promise, the future looking as bright as anyone could ask for, and still I wasn't at ease in the world.

We pulled into the parking area in front of the three-story stucco house in Crystal Meadows. I noted a battered pickup truck, not Hal Bell's. Mounted behind the cab was a black steel gun rack with rawhide ties at every bar. Stan Whitney hustled out the side door of the house and around the front of his SUV. He saw my car, stopped, threw a tasseled brown loafer over a front tire, stretched his hamstring and waved. Karen and I got out of the car. Stan headed in our direction. Wearing a white shirt and dark slacks, Stan's shoulders pressed forward like a man running with a football tucked under his arm.

He spoke rapidly. "Laura says you went to see Rattlesnake.

How is he?"

Karen said, "The usual upbeat Rattlesnake. He'd caught a rabbit. It made him happy to serve it to us in one of his stews."

Stan made a sour face. To me, he said, "What do you make of that hovel of a setup? Now that Dad's too out of it pursue his folly, something's got to be done. That's a lot of acreage to waste."

I said, "I think Rattlesnake's a great guy. As to what to do with the island, it's none of my business."

Stan's smile blazed. His teeth seemed freshly bleached. He had little time for us. "Well, you two have a good evening."

We said goodbye.

Stan turned and walked away. The SUV squawked at the unlocking of its doors. Stan grasped the handle. He looked over at Karen and me. "By the way, Aunty Rae is in town. She's back there with Dad right now. Whacko as ever."

Stan climbed in. The silver SUV started with a sound suggesting precision and power. It pulled forward from under the *porte cochere*, curved left around us, straightened and headed down the long driveway. Stan did not wave goodbye. I'd planted the tracking device under his vehicle late the night before.

"Your uncle doesn't exactly seem high on your Aunty Rae."

"She's not really anybody's aunt. She's my mom and uncle's cousin. The only daughter of Grandpa Clyde's youngest sister, who died thirty years ago."

"Why does Stan call her whacko?"

"I won't even try. Come on. Let's see if we can keep her from messing with Grandpa's head."

Karen moved with those gliding, level, gazelle-like strides. We went around the side of the house that Stan left from. We passed the patio furniture with fake kerosene lanterns, passed the swimming pool and tennis court. The door to Clyde's guesthouse was open, with the screen door closed. A brassy voice emanated, as did the smell of cigarette smoke.

Karen said, "Here goes," and opened the screen door.

We went inside. The screen door closed behind us with a hush. Seated in a plush dark chair, Clyde's stringy white hair looked to have been subjected to a whirlwind. His eyes followed the motions of a somewhat short woman in jeans, a green flannel cowboy shirt, and a brown leather belt flashing a gold buckle as bulbous as one on a prize fighter's championship belt. Her cigarette mowed the air like a barnstorming pilot showing off. Her hair was about equal parts mouse gray and steel wool. Curls rose and spewed in chaotic angles. At the sound of the screen door closing, the woman spun on black cowboy boots that showed wear like old tires. Metal caps were implanted in their toes.

Seeing Karen, her face brightened. "Why didn't anyone tell me you moved out West? I mean, come on, your Aunty Rae would've... I would've done something."

Karen said, "It's good to see you. It's been what, five years?"

Aunty Rae struck me as about fifty, roughly Stan Whitney's age by the calendar but with an extra ten thousand miles on the chassis. Wiry like the rest of the family, she advanced across the room on clumping boot heels. She switched the cigarette to her left hand. Her right reached out, not for Karen's hand but for mine. I gave her my right. She didn't seem to notice its lack of wholeness and she did not let go. Her breaths, exuding gin, sent a smell like the county dump in my direction.

"Karen Brady, is this the young man your Uncle Stanley says you're running around loose with?"

"Seeing each other, yes."

Karen took a lengthy step and plucked the burning cigarette from Aunty Rae's fingers. Aunty Rae didn't watch Karen cross the room and snuff it out in a saucer littered with cigarette butts. She looked me over. She wore thick round glasses. Between her teeth ran lines of gray.

Clyde stood up from his chair. As if remembering his manners, he said, "I'm Clyde Whitney. Welcome. These are two of my granddaughters, Karen and Rachel."

Aunty Rae groaned in frustration at Clyde's confusion about her name and how she was related to him.

Karen tended to Clyde, helping him sit back down. I heard her quietly ask if he was okay.

Aunty Rae spoke over her shoulder. "Karen dear, where do you get one of these? My goodness. TCH, as the sorority gals used to say. Tall, clean and handsome."

Karen came our way. She untangled my hand from Aunty Rae's. "You're making yourself look bad."

Aunty Rae's teeth disappeared. Her voice indicated she'd had plenty of nips from the gin bottle residing on the dining area table, next to a pack of cigarettes. "Now you be respectful of your elders. Do you hear me, little girl? Be respectful of your elders."

Clyde said, "I'm Clyde Whitney. We're safe here. But the safe is not safe."

Aunty Rae went to the table. She poured herself two inches of gin. "Why does he keep saying that?"

Clyde brushed back the white wisps hanging over his ears. He looked to Karen. "Do I know why?"

Karen guided the conversation to Aunty Rae, a subject she had no trouble warming to. She trained quarter horses, an hour south of Albuquerque. "Been in the business near twenty years. Won a lot of races. Won twice at Ruidoso Downs. You ever meet a woman horse trainer who's won all the big ones?"

I said, "I've never met any horse trainer. I once met the captain of a blimp. Also the last man to go over Niagara Falls locked in a barrel. I even had lunch with a guy who came in second at Nathan's Famous Hot Dog Eating Contest, on Coney Island. He didn't eat very much."

Aunty Rae's gray-lined teeth appeared again. She made a sharp poking motion with a finger, as if jabbing me in the ribs. "You got yourself a sense of humor. I like a man with a sense of humor."

Aunty Rae stepped to the pack of Camels on the table; Karen got there first, flicked the pack forward a couple of feet. "Outside, Aunty. You know the rules."

As if it were her house, Aunty Rae invited me to sit while she continued to talk about herself. She hadn't run what she referred to as her *boys* at the State Fair in Sacramento in a decade, but thought she'd check out the set up and consider bringing them north for the August races. Clyde's wan smile never ceased as his eyes roamed from speaker to speaker, with Karen feeding lines to the hard-drinking horsewoman. She let Aunty Rae talk herself out of breath.

Karen stood. "Grandpa likes to eat early. Katia puts his weekend meals in the refrigerator when she leaves on Friday."

In need of a cigarette, and maybe another drink, Aunty Rae picked up her gin and smokes. She looked to Karen. "Don't make a stranger of yourself. Stop by now and then."

Aunty Rae exited through the screen door.

Karen placed her hands atop her head. "Stop by now and then? I'm the one who's living here."

"Will she be staying in the main house?"

Clyde's face swiveled around, watching Karen and me.

Karen said, "They'd never allow it. There's always a fight. Whenever she visits someone, no one knows where she stays. She just pops in and out like a cuckoo clock."

74

Karen went to the main house. The screen door repeated its hushing sound. Clyde introduced himself to me again, put out a hand to shake. At giving him my chopped hand, he ran knobby fingers over the remaining stumps of mine. What seemed a river of warmth traveled through me. It lifted my spirits.

Karen heated a vegetarian quiche and cooked carrots, and washed two crisp red apples.

Clyde's eyes roamed the room as if in search of something. He said, "Everything has happened before. I'll remember doing something, while I'm doing it." Clyde seemed to search the room again. "Life goes on for billions of years. The universe collapses into a black hole. There's nothing. Then the big bang happens, and everything replays itself, over and over. It's an endless song."

Clyde looked to the ceiling. His whole being glowed.

"Everything is preordained, like being in a play."

This brought to mind the intense déjà vu I'd experienced on that first walk with Karen along the American River.

I said, "Those are interesting thoughts, Mr. Whitney."

He looked at me, eyes clear, bright, not blinking. "Are you here to take me above?"

Karen said, "Grandpa, this is Jeff. My boyfriend."

Clyde stood from the table. He wiped his right hand on his shirt, and extended it. "It's nice to meet you."

Eleven

Karen stayed with Clyde. I went to her place, sliced and mashed avocados and made guacamole to go with a bag of chips that had been left on the kitchen counter. An hour later, Karen and I shared this simple dinner, sitting across from each other at the oak coffee table.

Karen said, "You finding the wallet, which led to us meeting, do you think it could be fate? Like Grandpa talked about?"

"If this is fate," I said, "it's the best luck I've ever had."

"Be serious. What do you think?"

"I wouldn't dismiss anything Clyde says. He's been places the rest of us will never reach."

"Does it sound naïve? Thinking all this could be fate?"

"It sounds sincere."

Karen stood. "You know what? When I'm here, all I do is worry about Grandpa. Aunt Laura's home. Uncle Stan will check on him when he gets back. If he needs anything, Grandpa has his ringer for the house. It's by the bed. Let them check on him for one night. I want to sleep at your place."

Karen took out her phone, called her aunt and told Laura she was leaving for the night. Karen packed a small suitcase, and her green daypack with textbooks and notebooks. We left in my car. The diminishing light reminded me that summer's solstice was already a month past. Time itself had sped up with Karen in my life, activity at the medical center, keeping tabs on Hal Bell and Stan Whitney, and now thoughts of getting gold to put my financial house in order. I shook my head, to clear the competing thoughts, saw that other drivers had turned on headlights, and joined them.

My phone, in its holder, showed Stan Whitney's vehicle at his office, with him presumably in a business meeting even though it was Sunday evening. I pulled onto Highway 80 and headed toward downtown Sacramento. I raised the subject I'd been wanting to raise for days. "You told me to never hide things from you."

"I meant it."

"This is going to sound crass. Is your family rich?"

Karen said, "Compared to most people, yes, we're well off. No private jets or anything. There was family money. Most now is from a trust fund Grandpa set up after he sold his last patent." She reached back, pulled her ponytail around to her mouth. "My father managed to take a chunk of Mom's assets when he moved to France with his twenty-five-year-old secretary. He didn't even bother to say goodbye. I'll never forgive him."

We lurched along, slowed by summer's typical Sunday night traffic jam, people returning from Lake Tahoe and elsewhere in the mountains. Eight-thirty, darkness settling in, I opened a window for fresh air. Overlapping sounds of cars stopping and starting, the familiar sounds of a clogged highway, carried inside.

Karen said, "Anything else you want to know?"

I swallowed. "This is more of a confession."

"Sounds fun."

"It's not. I'm beginning to think too much about your grandfather's gold. I'm thinking I might end up paying for med school with it."

Karen said, "Thank you for telling me. And screw you for thinking like that."

The downtown exit was next. I flicked on the blinker. A tightness gripped my chest.

Karen said, "Do you feel better, now that you've told me?"

"I feel creepy."

Karen didn't say anything.

I said, "You say you'll never forgive your father for what he did. Do you think you can forgive me for thinking our relationship might help me financially?"

I glanced over. Karen looked out the passenger window.

Dark buildings, lining the freeway, blurred by. Neither of us spoke during the few minutes between the freeway exit and the bungalow. Headlights splashed across brown bricks. I cut the lights; the bricks disappeared. I reached to the backseat and grabbed the grocery bag we'd put the eight baggies of gold dust in. Karen got out of the car, slid on her daypack and snatched her small suitcase from the backseat. The only sound was buzzing from the freeway. With no porch light on, I fiddled with the key before getting the door unlocked. We stepped into a warm house that had been closed all day. I switched on the lights.

From the back of the house came what sounded like a drawer sliding. I took Karen's elbow.

"What now, Taylor?"

I put a finger to my lips. We ceased moving. I recognized the sound of the back door swinging open. I dropped the gold dust, ran through the living room, down the narrow hallway and out through the open door. I raced across the backyard.

Alleys run behind the houses in Sacramento's old neighborhoods. It used to be where you parked your buggy or wagon, later your car.

I ran through the opened back gate. To the right I heard footfalls, and took off. I made out a shadow moving away fast. I couldn't get a fix on the person fleeing. He or she had me by fifty feet. The head seemed a smooth oval, like it was covered with a knit cap. Forty feet. Thirty feet. A car in shadow. The driver's door swung out; faint light; the door slammed shut. The car's engine fired, coughing exhaust at me. I reached for the door handle. I grabbed it with my half hand.

The car peeled out, ripping my hand from the door handle. I lost footing and hit the hard-packed ground face first. The car's engine shifted gears rapidly. I rolled left and whipped out my phone. I zoomed in on the car and clicked pictures.

Behind me: "Jeff!"

At reaching the cross street, the car's lights came on. I clicked photos until it was gone. I got to my knees. Everything looked askew. My nose felt like it had been pumped full of air, then popped. The next thing I was aware of was Karen's arm going around my shoulder. She sat beside me on the dirt.

Karen said, "That car almost hit you."

"My hand's on fire."

"Where it was cut?"

I nodded, caught breath.

"Pinch your nose. You're bleeding."

I handed Karen my phone. Sticky blood covered part of its surface. I squeezed the tip of my nose together with thumb and forefinger. We walked toward my backyard. Karen coiled an arm around my middle. I listed rightward. She straightened my route.

Inside, I used a technique from my basketball days. If I got a bloody nose, I'd stuff a small wad of paper towel up it to staunch the bleeding, so I could stay in the game. The three baggies of gold dust I'd slipped under a binder in the bottom drawer of my desk, in the second bedroom, were missing. Whoever was there knew exactly what he was looking for, assuming it was a he. I grabbed a flashlight. Karen suggested I sit, calm down, and call the police.

The back door, as old as the house, still opened with a simple skeleton key; anybody could jiggle it ajar. I'd never worried about theft in the neighborhood, and, equally, I'd never had anything worth stealing. The back gate had a latch but no lock.

Carrying the flashlight in my left hand because my right hand hurt like it had been struck with a hammer, I went through the gate, swung the light back and forth. Progressing down the alley the direction I'd chased the shadow, I came upon a black latex glove, long enough to cover a hand and forearm, crumpled against the fence. It was turned inside-out. Another twenty feet and a second glove lay on the packed dirt. Thus vanished any hope of getting fingerprints. I ran the flashlight over everything to where the alley reached the cross street.

I returned home.

Karen made peppermint tea. She insisted I drink a cup. I said I'd found two gloves turned inside out. That the gloves showed dampness from sweating, and added that unlike saliva, sweat does not carry DNA. We sat on the couch in the living-dining area. Karen had wiped the blood off my phone, set it and the paper bag containing that day's catch of gold dust on the blonde Danish eating table. Adrenaline buzzed through me in irregular arcs.

Karen sat calmly with hands folded. When I finished rambling on, she took out her phone. "I got you the number of the police."

"If we tell them what was stolen, it'll raise questions. If we don't tell them what was stolen, and the cops find something that leads to finding the gold, how do we explain having the gold here in the first place?"

I couldn't sit still. I went to the kitchen, took a beer from the refrigerator. I uncapped it and downed a slug while walking back to the couch. I said, "This just got complicated. Somebody knew, or at least thought, we had some of your grandfather's gold."

"You think it's the guy from the white pickup?"

I downed another swallow of cold beer. "This person seemed smaller. I can't even say for sure it was a male. I hope it's the same guy. Last thing we need is two people to worry about. Tomorrow I'll have a locksmith install new locks, with dead bolts. I'll get a bulb for the backyard light. I'll get a lock for the gate. I—"

"Should probably slow down." Karen reached across the couch, ran a hand down my arm. "Jeff, the chase is over."

I spied my phone on the dining area table. "I want to look at the pictures I took. They're probably unreadable, but maybe I got lucky."

Karen said, "Then it's ice for your hand, and we take a look at your nose. No arguing."

I went into the second bedroom, retrieved my notably not-stolen laptop. The biggest question roiling through me was how did the thief come to think there might be gold hidden in the brick bungalow? And how did he or she connect me to Clyde Whitney's mining efforts in the first place?

Taking the laptop to the dining table, I asked Karen to join me. I emailed the phone photos to myself. I brought them onscreen. The first four were no clearer than the shadow I'd chased down the alley. The last three, however, with the car lights on, dimly showed the license plate. I brightened the contrast. Karen and I took turns using a magnifying glass. We could make a reasonable guess at a number 5, and a letter A. Otherwise, the numbers and letters were indecipherable. What stuck out was the background, not the white of a regular California license plate.

"That's a Nevada plate."

"How do you know?"

"See that blue, like a sky? That's the tip-off. The other is three numbers followed by three letters. Lots of Nevada plates are like that. It doesn't do us much good, but it's a start."

"He would come all the way from Nevada?"

"Not necessarily. Sometimes guys use stolen plates. Use them once, toss them in a dumpster."

"Now that you've calmed down, what do you think about calling the police? Report the robbery. What if this person comes back?"

I said, "You'd get into an awful spot with family members if they know we found and kept gold from them."

"All they can really do is get mad. I'm more interested in feeling safe."

"Short term, unless the guy—let's assume it was a guy—was hired by your aunt and uncle, he got roughly eighteen thousand dollars' worth of gold. He's not going to contact your family members about it. We'll put the rest in my locker at the med center. People go in and out all day. My locker's always locked."

The orange flecks in Karen's eyes seemed brighter than usual. She made fists and bounced them off her knees. "Let's get some ice on that hand of yours."

Twelve

Karen on the couch, me at the dining table with my hand in a bowl of ice cubes, I phoned Clint Sherman. I told him everything that transpired, and asked if he thought I should call the police.

Clint said, "Do you believe someone might harm you or Karen?"

"I'm rattled, but not scared. The guy in the truck could've stomped the crap out of me. He didn't. Tonight, I'm pretty sure it was a different person. This guy doesn't scare me at all."

"With the first incident, you don't have any info other than a white pickup truck, of which there are millions. Tonight, it looks like no chance for fingerprints. If you call the police, it'll bring attention to, let's call it the extracurricular activities you and Karen are indulging in with the gold."

"I take it you don't approve."

"I don't approve or disapprove, as long as you are confident you're both not in physical jeopardy. Whoever's behind this knows about Karen. Keep her safety in mind when deciding whether or not to do something."

We were having the kind of father-son conversation I'd never had with anybody other than Clint Sherman.

I said, "I hear you."

"Email me the pictures. I'll have someone with better equipment take a look." I pictured Clint walking, slightly stooped, back and forth across the dark wood floor in the living room of his 1920s Arts and Crafts style home. "I don't have much hope for the photos. I'll call as soon as I hear anything."

We said goodbyes. I clicked off, set the phone on the table.

Karen said, "Well, what did he say?"

"He told me to be sure to use protection tonight."

Karen snatched a brown end pillow from the couch, hopped up and hit me in the back with it. "You're impossible."

Her swat caused me to spill icy water from the bowl. "How can that be? I'm coming around to Clyde's way of thinking. If everything's happened before, that means I'm not impossible. I'm inevitable."

Karen gave me a playful shove. "I still say you're impossible."

"Clint agrees with me. We have no evidence to give the police. The only result reporting tonight will be drawing attention to our keeping something that didn't belong to us. Plus they'll want to know if we have more. You know? Clint's exception to this way of thinking is, if we're in physical danger, we call the police."

"Are we in danger?"

"I don't think either of the two parties want to hurt us. If they did, they would've done so already."

Lumber yards open early. I rolled into Kiefer's Wood Products at six a.m., bought lengths of Douglas fir cylinders an inch in diameter, a tape measure and a handsaw. Once home, I left a message with a locksmith. Left another on Dr. Fisher's phone, telling him I wouldn't be in till after his lunch. Karen walked the thirty minutes to the medical center. I sawed the rounds of Douglas fir into lengths to fit in the window frames while closed, so when in place it would not be possible to slide the windows open.

A genial guy named Jerry Diaz arrived. He said he hadn't seen door locks as useless as those on the bungalow's doors in years. Diaz installed new locks and dead bolts on the front and back doors. They worked with the same key. He put a padlock on the backyard gate latch. I added to my Visa card debt.

Shortly after one o'clock, after securing the eight baggies of gold dust in my medical center locker, I joined Dr. Fisher on his rounds. I was only half aware of the patients. My mind kept returning to the gold dust, and the two encounters with people whose faces I hadn't been able to see. Karen texted she wanted to go to Crystal Meadows to check on Clyde. We met in the medical center parking lot. I gave her a new door key. We headed out under inexhaustible Sacramento Valley sun.

As we entered the Whitney compound, a sleek gold Porsche reflected that sun. I went to Karen's guesthouse. She went to check on Clyde. About two minutes later, Karen came in.

"Was there a note on my door?"

"No. Why?"

"Grandpa's not here. If anyone takes him somewhere, they're supposed to leave a note on the front door of the house, and on my door. That's how we let each other know where he is."

"Maybe somebody just forgot."

Karen tugged my elbow. "Let's see who's around."

We went to the back door, pressed the bell. An orchestral bonanza rang out. Housekeeper Katia answered.

She said, "I was just about to leave."

Karen said, "Is my Aunt Laura home?"

"She's with a visitor, upstairs."

Katia shut the door on us. Karen tried the knob: locked. Late afternoon sun bounced hotly off the back wall of the house.

Karen said, "I don't trust Katia."

"You don't trust anyone who's around your grandfather. It's getting so I don't, either."

Laura Whitney opened the chocolate brown back door. She invited us in. Dressed in another mix of whites, she introduced Karen and me to Niki Papadopoulos, about forty, shiny dark hair and shiny dark eyes. The color of her sleek pantsuit matched the olive color of her skin. Niki wore an array of gold jewelry as extensive as Laura's twinkling diamonds.

Laura said, "She's my bestie."

Niki's face flashed like she was posing for a photograph.

Karen told Laura that Clyde was not in his guesthouse, and no note was on her door or the front door about him being elsewhere. "Do you know where he is?"

Laura said, "You sure he's not on the property? Aunty Rae gave him a full day. She drove him up to Tahoe for lunch. She couldn't have left here more than half an hour ago." Laura turned to Niki. "About half an hour, right?"

Niki said, "Maybe closer to an hour."

I said, "Did you actually see Clyde?"

Laura said, "I didn't need to. Katia informed me when Aunty Rae and Clyde returned. Like she is supposed to."

Karen said, "Do you know where Aunty Rae is now?"

"We don't even have her cell. She's a woman of mystery. A woman of rudeness and mystery."

Laura said she and Niki would search the grounds.

Niki said, "That'll be nifty. I've never actually seen the whole place."

I wondered if they would tote parasols.

Karen's frustration showed. Still, she kept her cool. "We'll drive around the neighborhood. I'll report him missing."

Laura smiled effortlessly, reminding me of husband Stan. "We don't want any police cars here. That's not a good look. If they say they're coming, tell them to use an unmarked car. Don't be afraid to throw the family name around."

Karen said, "Whatever," and headed back to her place, sliding her phone out from a back pocket of her jeans.

We took the Jetta. At the end of the driveway, Karen pointed right. I said, "Why this way?"

"It's the way you go to the hospital, Grandpa's house, Hal Bell's, places that in short spurts he remembers."

Out of habit I placed my phone in its holder, tapped it to check on Stan Whitney. Nothing unusual. I said, "When I used to look for people who disappeared, I'd pretend to be them. Try to be inside their heads. You and Clyde ever go for walks?"

"Sometimes. After he had dinner, and the heat let up. He's still pretty nimble."

"What did he talk about?"

"You know Grandpa. One minute he'll talk about some incredible trip he took forty years ago, the next he's off in space somewhere."

"Anything you can remember might help."

We drove along blocks of manicured grounds and stucco McMansions. Karen's phone buzzed. Missing Persons returning her call. Karen was told an officer would be at 3134 Ralston Avenue in fifteen minutes. Karen clicked off. She called Laura and said to expect the police. Again, she clicked off.

Karen said, "Willow Pond."

"Willow Pond?"

"I just remembered. Once when we were out walking, he asked if I'd ever been blessed by the shade at Willow Pond."

"Do you know where it is?"

"We never went there." Karen lifted her phone. "I'll search

willow, pond, Crystal Meadows California."

Keeping an eye out for Clyde, I made a turn. We passed a corner estate with a renovated Conestoga wagon set on a stone platform. Cleanly painted, the canvas cover pristine, I figured a maintenance worker was stuck with keeping the wagon forever young. How many people could eat with the money tossed at that old wagon?

I made another turn.

Karen said, "Got it." She lifted her phone to in front of her eyes. "It's actually Willow Park. Point-eight miles. Go straight half a mile. I'll let you know when to turn left.

A one-lane road ran between the back fences of more McMansions. It ended at an empty parking lot that could accommodate twenty cars. A sign read *WILLOW PARK*. Under that was *Crystal Meadows Owners Association*. There was a horseshoe pit with a rake propped against one of the backboards. The pond, about an acre, was surrounded by neatly trimmed lawn. Closer to the parking spaces than the water, old growth willow trees reigned over picnic tables like massive green umbrellas. Clyde Touhy Whitney sat at one, facing the water. At that angle, snowy hair covering his ears and falling over the collar of his dark shirt, he reminded me of a bald eagle.

Clyde didn't turn when Karen and I shut car doors. It was quiet out, not a ripple on the pond. Perhaps that prompted our not speaking until we went around the table and sat across from Clyde. His eyes were teary.

Karen said, "Grandpa, what's wrong?"

"Nothing." Clyde spoke softly. "Everything's perfect, all the time." He raised his thin arms and looked up. "Can you feel it?" His eyes fell to Karen and me. "Don't think. Touch the table."

The words carried a hypnotic quality. I touched the table. Its warmth, in the shade of the ancient willow tree, was genuinely perfect. I saw veins in the skinny willow branches pulsating, breathing, green even in the sweltering, late-July heat.

Karen said, "Yes. I see."

I said, "Me, too."

Clyde said, "I sense your minds move too fast to truly see. Every tree, bird, face, cloud. Everything should be received separately. That's how you truly see them."

I think Karen, too, was mesmerized by Clyde's tender words. His gaze seemed to see far ahead, and inward at the same time.

Clyde turned to me. "Why is it so hard to go?"

"I don't know. You know more about these things than most of us."

Clyde said, "I'm ready to meet my maker. I brought an offering." He reached into a pocket of his jeans and pulled out a Ziploc baggy half-filled with gold dust. "Every day I hear the call. Still, I am here. Why am I still here?"

The word *here* seemed to prompt something in Clyde's mind. He seemed confused. "When did I get back from the mine?"

Karen said, "Aunty Rae took you to Lake Tahoe for lunch."

Clyde's face grew cloudy. "Is that true? I don't remember seeing the lake."

Karen said, "Don't worry about it. We're just happy we found you. Let's get you home."

Clyde's hands rose again, palms up, as if in benediction. "You're an old soul, Caroline."

He got up from the bench with an effort that sapped him. Clyde's movements were uncharacteristically slow. His face looked like it had seen too much sun for one day. Karen hurried to his side and took Clyde's elbow just as he began to wobble. We headed for the car.

Clyde said, "Practice quiet. Don't let your mind run about."

*

That night, in bed, awake while Karen slept, I reflected on the man who sat peacefully under willow trees, who seemed equal parts of this world and otherworldly. Clyde conveyed zero ego, zero sense of self-importance. Being around him steered me back to things I hadn't thought about since childhood.

As a lonely boy hanging out in redwood trees taller than cathedrals, I made up a mind game I called Disappear. Walking in the unbroken shade of trees that emerged from the ground before Columbus sailed to the Americas, I'd stop, and sit on a bed of soft moist redwood needles and rotting bark bits. I'd take a fallen branch and smooth the duff into a flat surface. With each breath I took in the rich clean scent of a virgin redwood forest.

I drew, making a circle for the sun, smaller circles for the planets, all the way out to Pluto. I'd close my eyes and let blackness slowly grow around me, like a cocoon. I'd say: "There is no world." Focusing on imagined space, I'd follow my breaths in, and out, in, and out, until a blue earth vanished from among the planets. It was like falling into a trance. "There is no solar system." I'd focus, not fighting intruding thoughts, minute after uncounted minute, until blackness sifted through me, replacing the sun and the planets. It was as if I floated in a place somewhere between earth and above. Eventually, I lost any sense of arms, legs, or body. Then: "There are no stars." After a while, blackness coated me. Inside and out, blackness. Finally: "There is nothing." I'd wait for the thought to grow within. "There is nothing." Finally, the blackness, too, disappeared. "There is nothing."

I'd slip into a black void. I disappeared. Nothing existed. For how long, I never knew. I'd wake up, a boy alone in shadowy woods. I'd run through the moist forest, thinking I'd disappeared during the unaccounted-for time. That was the ritual's tantalizing allure. At nine and ten years old, I believed my passages into nothingness gave my life a spooky magic I would never fully understand.

I wondered if Clyde understood traveling from life into nothingness, and back into life. If his mind had still been intact, I would have asked.

Thirteen

Tuesday morning, Karen went to class. I called the number Bob Williams had given her. I didn't know where or how to look into who else was after Clyde's gold, so I did what Clint Sherman taught me: when stuck, go back to the beginning. I asked Bob if he planned on being home for the day.

"Since I retired, every day's Saturday. I'll be here loafing."

"Want me to pick up anything on the way?"

Bob said, "Two cases of Coors Light wouldn't dampen my spirits." He burst into merriment. "We're set just fine. You like toasted cheese sandwiches?"

I packed water and snacks, double-checked the windows and back door, locked the front door and headed for Pine Grove. I glanced in the rearview mirror frequently. I stopped at a Rotten Robbie gas station and filled the tank.

A leisurely drive took me through the turns and small towns of Highway 49.

Bob Williams shook my hand and shot me the same no-nonsense look as the other time we'd met. He seemed pleased to have company. The round outdoor table with an umbrella was set with plates, and white paper napkins held down by drinking glasses. Bob wore what I'm certain was the same overalls as before. Its pouch bulged. The day was mercifully cool, smelling of pine trees. Somewhere out of sight a wind chime sang amiably. Darlene brought out four steaming toasted cheese sandwiches enhanced with sliced pickles and finely chopped white onions. She scooped two onto each plate. Bob went to a bucket and plucked us dripping silver cans of Coors Light. I declined the one he pushed to the middle of the table. It was ten-thirty in the morning.

"Okay," Bob said. "What can I do you for?"

I told Bob a couple of lies. I said that after Karen and I left his house, we were followed by an oversized white pickup. "All the way to Sacramento." The next lie was that two nights before, I noticed somebody nosing around in front of my house. "When I went outside, he took off. I wasn't able to catch him."

I added, "We know somebody broke into Clyde's house, and turned it inside-out. Looking for what must be gold. The guy the other night, it could be a coincidence. Except to say Clyde Whitney spent twenty years mining, and far as anybody knows, he never sold an ounce. Common sense tells me people are after whatever stash he may have. I'm trying to figure out what's going on before someone gets hurt. Basically, Karen or me."

Bob set down a toasted cheese sandwich emitting its last puffs of steam. He fished out his thick, black-rimmed glasses, and set them on his even thicker, red-veined nose. He looked toward the road crossing in front of his driveway. "Funny you come here today." Bob pointed to the asphalt road that angled slightly downhill at passing his property. "Yesterday, I'm fixing turkey sandwiches for me and the Mrs." He pointed. "You hear a car when it comes over the hill. Out of habit, I look up. For a second, I think I see Clyde Whitney in the passenger seat. It was just a blink. I didn't think much of it."

"What kind of car?"

"A pickup."

"White?"

Bob took off his glasses, clicked the frames closed and slipped them into the pouch of his denim overalls. "I don't know. It was just a blink." He ran a hand across his thick mustache; it made a rustling sound. "I didn't think to call anybody, figuring someone would call me if Clyde went missing. Did he go missing?"

"He was with a relative most of yesterday. Up at Tahoe. Then with Karen and me through dinner."

We went back to consuming melted cheese, toasted bread and trimmings.

I said, "How about the house? Anything unusual?"

"Only thing unusual is you coming up here today. Listen, mister, no nonsense. Why did you come up here on your own? No Karen Brady."

I told Bob that Karen was in class at the UC Medical Center, and that I was on the level.

Bob took out his thick glasses, put them on again and looked to the road. "Maybe it *was* Clyde in that pickup." The glasses clicked closed and disappeared. "Not likely, right? You say he's accounted for all day."

I nodded. Bob popped open the second can of beer. Hissing foam burbled over his thumb.

Bob said, "You telling me about being followed, and someone poking around outside your house, I'm thinking something screwy's going on."

"I'm trying to determine if it's all a coincidence, or not."

We finished the early lunch. We shook hands and said goodbye. I swung onto Red Corral Road and proceeded in the same loop Karen and I took, heading down to Pine Grove, turning right and climbing elevation into sweet-smelling forest. Another right dropped me to the Mokelumne River. I slowed on turns and didn't see anyone following me. I pulled in at the gate to Watters Mine. I tapped the code Clyde had handed Karen, written on a slip of paper, after we found him reaching for the sky.

The gate shut behind me. I wasn't worried about Bob Williams showing up. The walk from his house to the mine was half a mile, steep, and he was likely on beer number four or five. Besides, my car couldn't be seen from Red Corral Road.

I parked. I walked uphill on the side road I'd seen the other time I was there. It led to the original Watters Mine, a cave carved into the hillside. I turned on my flashlight and went in. Timbers framed the ceiling. I heard water dripping—and stepped into a puddle. The timbers were so rotted I dislodged a chunk by merely touching one. I got out of there fast.

Back at the car, I gathered up a screwdriver, wrench and a crowbar. The tin warehouse-like edifice was to the left. To the right, small wood structures. They were locked. I went to work. Eight screws dropped to the ground. I pulled a latch out of its engraved position in dull Douglas fir boards, yanked the door open. I grabbed my square flashlight and stepped inside. The air stale, it obviously hadn't been opened in a long time, possibly years. I touched the ceiling, feeling my way along wood rafters for hidden Ziploc baggies. Shelves held tools. Several I didn't recognize.

I worked all afternoon. My hand was sore but not painful. I made a deep ding in one of the wood doors. Who would ever notice? By the time I got to the big metal building, I was past worrying about creating evidence of my snooping. I ripped off a rusted lock and pushed open the metal door. I reached into shadows searching for Ziploc baggies. When finished, I slid the metal door shut. I leaned a chunk of iron pipe against the door. If anyone entered the building, he or she would have to move it. I'd be able to see that a slash mark near its top was no longer hidden against the metal *'handed face'*

door. I drove home sore handed and empty handed, looking into the rearview mirror more than was rational.

At the brick bungalow, I checked the windows and back door. No signs of meddling. Karen came after her classes. She kissed me on the lips.

"How'd it go?"

Rather than sharing the brown couch, we sat across from each other. I recounted the early lunch with Bob Williams. And Bob thinking he saw Clyde whizz by about noon the day before, in a pickup truck he didn't identify as white. "I think your Aunty Rae may have taken Clyde to the mine, not Tahoe. That explains his asking how long he'd been away from it."

"I'd like to grill her on that."

I didn't respond.

Karen said, "Well?"

"Since we can't prove anything one way or the other, I think it's better not to tip our hand. Don't put her on guard. If she's on guard, she's less apt to slip up."

"I don't think you like confronting people. I think you avoid conflict as much as possible."

"I'd like to point out your field is elder care, not psychiatry."

"I'm just saying."

I described breaking into the wood structures. I described the inside of the warehouse-sized metal structure. "It's basically the same as the one on the island."

"Okay. Enough throat clearing. How many did you find?"

"Nada."

"Don't joke with me. You searched everywhere. How many baggies get added to the collection?"

My palms opened. "I'm not joking. I didn't find any."

Karen got up and walked into the kitchen. I heard water from the faucet. She returned sipping from a glass. "You expect me to believe you? Everywhere we've gone, we find more baggies. They're like gopher holes. The more you look, the more you see."

Heat prickled my face. "You know what? This gold dust is making us nuts." I stood. "I'm paranoid. You think I'm lying. If you want, I'll go to the med center and bring you the eight baggies. Have a snack and I'll bring you the gold right now."

Karen didn't look at me. She said, "I think I should go."

I said, "Okay. Goodbye." I walked down the hallway to my bedroom, and shut the door. I heard the front door shut. My mind raced. Did Karen want the gold even more than I? Had she been using me? Why else would a woman like Karen Brady fall for me, no close friends, no family, a chip on my shoulder the size of a basketball?

The usual cure for this condition was a three-mile run. I locked the back door on the way out, went down the alley and broke into a jog.

Three blocks later, I stopped. This was crazy. I'd done nothing wrong and there I was, as usual, telling myself I didn't deserve what I wanted: Karen Brady's love.

Karen had acted completely out of character. What brought it on?

On Wednesday it was a relief to have duties at the medical center. Dr. Fisher had me begin the routine exams. Then he asked questions of the patients in a way that was a teaching technique. Before he left for the day, he gave me pointers on how to get children to talk about their health.

Thursday was harder. I took two three-mile runs. I lifted weights. No text or call from Karen. All I got from my phone was knowledge that Stan drove to San Francisco. My mind seemed about to burst, worrying about Karen, the guy who'd broken into my house, and wondering who the driver of the white pickup was. How was Clyde doing?

Clint called. The photos I'd taken with my phone had yielded nothing more than my one supposition: a Nevada license plate.

Friday morning Dr. Fisher had a visitor, a partner in his medical practice before Dr. Fisher joined the staff at the university. Dr. Al Oppenheim was Dr. Fisher's height and age, but his opposite otherwise. He had a shaved head, thick shoulders. He talked fast and made quips at every opportunity. He was widely considered one of the finest pediatricians in the Sacramento Valley.

The three of us headed off to see a patient Dr. Oppenheim wanted Dr. Fisher's impressions of. My phone, sound turned off, vibrated in a front pocket. Normally I didn't check who was calling. I checked.

"I should take this."

Doctors Oppenheim and Fisher walked farther down the hall, stopped at where another hallway crossed it. I clicked my phone. No way was I going to say I was sorry.

"Hello."

"Grandpa's gone again. I went to check on him, before going to class. He wasn't there." Karen's words spilled rapidly. "We've looked everywhere. Aunt Laura's driving the streets. I'm on foot. County police has a car out."

"I'm on my way."

I jogged down the hall, told Dr. Fisher an emergency had come up and was moving before he had a chance to respond. I hustled through the building. Jogging past the security guard, I gave him a wave. I had to slow, to wait for the automatic glass doors to swoosh open.

Outside, I sprinted.

Fourteen

I rolled up the long driveway. Karen waited at the steps in front of the main house. I parked between it and the four-car garage. Karen hurried toward me before I could get out, arms wide, eyes wild. "I don't know what got into me the other day. I kind of do, but—"

"What do you know about Clyde?"

Karen flung open the passenger door, jumped in. She understood we'd discuss our argument later. "Like I said, when I went to check on him this morning, he wasn't there. I called Aunt Laura. She hadn't seen him. Neither had Katia."

"What do the police say?"

"Nobody's seen anything."

As Clint Sherman was a replacement for the father I'd never met, Clyde Whitney was becoming the grandfather figure I'd always longed to know. Plus, he represented those aspects of life that soared beyond the everyday. I had to find him.

I said, "Tell me everything."

In short, Clyde was gone without a trace. I kissed Karen on the forehead, and sat back. I closed my eyes and did my best to be inside Clyde Whitney's head. I'm awake, alone in the guesthouse, thinking of what comes after life on earth.

"I assume you checked Willow Park."

"Aunt Laura did, while I've been walking the streets. The police went there, too."

I pressed everything I associated with Clyde together in my mind. I said, "Let's go to Willow Park."

"I told you. They've already been."

I looked at Karen's unsettled face. "I love you."

Karen said, "You're strange. But don't you dare change."

I said, "You saw how he glowed under that willow tree. I think he goes to Willow Park first. Maybe he left a clue."

We drove to Willow Park, looking down every side street and driveway along the way. I tried to be Clyde Whitney. A part of me wished I *were* Clyde Whitney, that I had his gentle love for whatever was in front of him. I concocted the irrational thought of Clyde moving in with me and Karen, in the brick bungalow. A certain kind of upbringing breeds a certain neediness. It makes you want things that are pure fantasy.

Karen and I rolled down the narrow road between the backyards of Crystal Meadows McMansions. At Willow Park, one car reflected glare under sun in the parking lot. A tan sedan. My mind jumped to the fleeing speedster, but the only person in sight was an octogenarian at a table enjoying the shade of an ancient willow tree. Gray as a cloudy day, he worked at consuming a sandwich. Karen and I got out of the car.

Karen said, "I'll talk to him. You're too wound up. You'll scare him off."

She headed for the picnic table. I walked the lush grass surrounding the pond, trying to be Clyde. What am I thinking? Where do I go?

My eyes combed the grass.

Karen approached from the side. "Find anything?"

"Not a leaf."

Karen said, "That man's only been here ten minutes. He didn't see Grandpa, or anybody."

I said, "We have to be thorough. I'll be right back." I went to my car. From the backseat I took binoculars and the big flashlight. I marched toward the pond.

Karen said, "Jeff, don't think that."

"I'm sorry."

Karen, ponytail bobbing, curled back around in a half circle. She pulled out her phone and tapped numbers while walking to the car. I went to the pond. I put eyes to binoculars. I surveyed the pond. Steadying the binoculars with my good left hand, I flicked on the flashlight with my right and ran its light over the water's surface.

Light from the powerful flashlight penetrated the water for what I estimated as three feet. I walked the shore, shining the light from the edge of the grass to about a fourth of the way across the cloudy pond, maybe less. Beyond that, the light didn't penetrate the surface. I had to be sure Clyde Whitney wasn't in there. I had to know he was wandering the streets of Crystal Meadows in the warming day. I wanted to spend more hours with him.

A dozen feet from shore, something in the water looked pink. Whatever it was, it seemed to semi-float a few feet under the surface. It wasn't pink. Light colored, it was attached to something darker that disappeared in deeper water. My heart pounded blood into my head like I'd been shot full of dope.

The light color was a shoe.

I got out my phone and dialed 9-1-1. I told the person who answered where I was, what I had seen, and gave her my name.

I joined Karen in the car. As gently as I could, I told her what I'd seen.

She said, "Are you sure?"

My right arm went around her shoulder.

Karen tucked her head under my chin. For once in my life, I kept my mouth shut, just let moments be themselves.

"Is it possible it's someone else?"

My response was to pull Karen across the middle of the front seat and hug her.

I said, "I'm lucky to have met him."

We held each other in silence until the rising howls of a siren invaded the open car windows. It grew louder. It was joined by a second howling. A county police car, followed by a boxy white ambulance, pulled into the parking lot. The octogenarian had driven off. Perhaps the approaching sirens spurred him into going home.

Karen said, "Could you talk to them? Please?"

I got out and met a woman and a man, both about thirty, wearing metal badges. Two men in matching white uniforms stayed back at the ambulance. One leaned against a headlight. The other put a walkie-talkie to his mouth and spoke into it.

The female deputy said, "Are you the individual who called 911?" Her hair dwelled under a patrolman's cap. Her voice was low, intent.

I said I'd made the call.

"Show us why."

I walked the officers to where I'd left the flashlight and binoculars. The woman deputy pointed to the binoculars. "May I?"

"Of course."

She picked them up, put her eyes to the two slots.

I grabbed the flashlight and snapped it awake. I aimed it at the area I'd seen a shoe and what I took to be a pants leg. "Ten or twelve feet out, you'll see something light colored that runs into something dark colored."

The woman deputy stepped to water's edge, tilted the binoculars, found the spreading circle of light from the flashlight. She turned the left focusing dial, turned it back a bit. She turned the right focusing dial, and flinched. She said to her partner, "Get Lieutenant Burns. Tell him we got a body."

The male deputy moved away and spoke into a tiny microphone at the end of a black wire that ran out of the left front pocket of his thick uniform shirt.

The woman officer said, "Let me see your ID." I fished out my wallet. She gave my butchered hand a double take. She looked over my driver's license. "Who's the lady in the car?"

"The granddaughter of who I think is in the pond. Karen Brady. Her grandfather's name is Clyde Whitney."

"And you are?"

"Karen's boyfriend."

"Okay. Sit tight till the boss gets here."

"I'll be in the car."

She gave me my wallet. "How's she holding up?"

"It hasn't really hit her yet. Excuse me," I said, and headed for the car. "I should be with her."

Lieutenant John Burns arrived in an unmarked car. He clambered out, hitched his slacks and went straight to the woman deputy. She gave him a salute, as did the male deputy who stood by the pond, looking through the binoculars. I got out of the car and walked toward the trio of police.

Burns snapped at the deputy who had the binoculars. "Put those down. Show some respect."

The deputy bent at the knees, let go of the binoculars. He stepped away from them to between the pond and Lieutenant Burns.

Burns' eyes were dark marbles. He wore a navy blue tie, white shirt, dark slacks and shiny black shoes.

Burns said, "What made you come here?"

"Karen's grandfather has, or had, latter stage dementia. Sometimes he wanders off. A few days ago we found him sitting under one of these willow trees. He was completely lost."

Burns nodded in a way that conveyed suspicion. "On the way, I talked to the officers who've been looking for him. They say they told Mr. Whitney's daughter-in-law they'd checked the park. She said she herself checked here earlier. Everybody was in communication. It doesn't make sense for you to come here."

"I'm just telling you what happened."

Burns said, "Were you here early this morning? What about in the middle of the night?"

"Last night I was home. In downtown Sacramento. I went to the UC medical center at nine this morning." Tense, I moved my body around. The inference that I'd harm Clyde angered me. "There are plenty of witnesses."

Burns' eyes moved. I followed his gaze to the parking lot. Stan Whitney's Mercedes SUV crossed the lot at a good clip. He parked sideways rather than pull into one of the striped parking spaces. The driver's door opened, Stan hopped out and trotted across the grass in a crisp dark suit and flapping red tie. I thought of him running the bases after belting a home run. His blond hair, parted on the left, did not betray its artful composition. Without slowing Stan produced a white business card and flashed it at Lieutenant Burns and the female deputy. He reached the three of us, sensed who was in charge and thrust the business card into the lieutenant's right hand.

"Stan Whitney. Good to meet you."

Burns looked at the card. Stan placed himself between Burns and me. He turned his back to the lieutenant.

Stan whispered, "He'll try to mess with you. I've seen him in action, after we had a break-in at a construction site."

Lieutenant Burns said, "If you don't mind, I'm trying to do my job."

Stan turned toward Burns. "I do mind. Jeff is a friend of the family. Now tell me what you know about my dad. And why—assuming he's in there—why haven't you gotten him out yet?"

A fire truck roared into the lot. No siren. The huge red machine heaved to a loud airbrakes-hissing stop. Directly behind it came a white pickup truck with county insignia splashed across its sides. Two men hopped out and went to the truck's bed. They wore black wetsuits. Lieutenant Burns didn't speak for a few seconds. He seemed overloaded with people to boss around. The two newly arrived guys fetched oxygen tanks and jogged toward the knot of us standing on spongy grass. Rather than shoes, they wore webbed rubber booties.

One called ahead, "Sorry. We were dragging for another in the American."

Stan's face grew the Whitney frown. His eyes scrunched together. Stan headed for the Jetta.

Lieutenant Burns said, "Where do you think you're going?"

Stan spoke loudly over a thick shoulder. "I probably just lost my father. My niece probably just lost her grandfather. Why don't you go piss up a hose and inhale the steam?"

PART TWO

Fifteen

The coroner's report listed Clyde's cause of death as accidental drowning. The inquest made note of his latter-stage dementia. It stated that acute dementia likely made Clyde disoriented after he fell into the water, because it appeared he stepped toward the pond's middle rather than back toward shore. The autopsy revealed no marks on the body, therefore no signs of a struggle. No drugs were detected, and there was no evidence suggesting Clyde Whitney took his own life.

To me, it seemed the survival instinct would have kicked in. That Clyde, who Stan said was a good swimmer when young, would have tried to get back to shore. The assumption that Clyde fell in was questionable in that we had no knowledge of him ever walking along the pond's edge. His haven was sitting beneath the enormous willow trees, closer to the parking lot than the water.

The idea that Clyde hadn't slipped in, and that someone drowned him, didn't wash because drowning Clyde eliminated the possibility of him leading the killer to gold—unless he, or she, had gotten Clyde to reveal a hiding place. But with Clyde's mind as wavering as it was, why bank on anything he said as being accurate?

Karen wanted to move on. Me, too. I couldn't.

The evening before the inquest report was made public, I heard a vehicle park on the street at my place. Through the kitchen window I saw a large white pickup under draping branches of the sycamore in my front yard. I went to my bedroom closet. I'd put an aluminum baseball bat in it that was left in the garage by the previous tenant. I'd practiced swinging it every night since Clyde Whitney's presence in my life brought threats, real and imagined. I knew I could do damage with that bat.

The driver's door opened. Out came a man who moved on the balls of his feet. Alarm bells rang inside me. I went to the front door. I stood where I'd be hidden if it were forced open. I told myself to slam the bat into his balls.

Nothing.

I hurried to the kitchen. Through the window I caught taillights of the big white pickup motoring away. Across the street, facing the opposite direction, lights came on in a big sedan, its color masked by the darkness of night. The car went forward, then made a U-turn that crossed the end of my driveway. I couldn't see anything except the shoulders and neck of the driver. The dark sedan moved in the direction of the white Ram 2500.

I went outside. Silence except the buzz that sailed from the freeway at all hours.

With the body released by the county, Karen, Stan and Laura accompanied Clyde on a flight East for him to be buried next to his beloved Joanie. Karen and I discussed me accompanying her. We thought it not a suitable time to meet her mom, brother Sam and other family members. It could wait.

Katia used the Whitneys' departure as a chance to take a week off. Stan asked me to stay at the compound and keep an eye on things. He didn't offer to pay, which I took as recognition that I'd be insulted. I removed the Sherman Investigations pistol from beneath the driver's seat, and deposited my car at a downtown repair shop to get an oil change, tune up, and have the radiator flushed. I borrowed Karen's Volvo.

On Monday I returned from the medical center and wandered the expansive grounds, thinking about Clyde. He'd been a person of the spirit and not the material, except for gold, which he'd never swapped for money. In terms of physicians, I wanted to become more like Dr. Fisher. In terms of people, the desire to become more like Clyde increased after his passing.

Tuesday night at the Whitney compound, I went for a moonlit swim. I left the pool lights off. The heated water made agreeable, soothing, splashing sounds as I swam laps. This had a cleansing effect.

The next night, when I went out to swim in darkness, I saw light beyond the tennis court, in the back right quadrant of the compound, the guesthouse where Clyde had lived his last months. I returned to the other guesthouse, got dressed and went to the trunk of Karen's Volvo. Its toolbox yielded a substantial wrench.

I walked to the partly lighted guesthouse. I peered through a side window. Didn't see anyone. I went to the entry door, listened. Nothing. I hoisted the wrench, pulled back the screen door, turned the handle of the entry door and stepped inside. I held the wrench high, hoping to scare somebody enough that I wouldn't need to use it. The screen door hushed as it closed behind me.

From a back bedroom: "Mister Bell?"

A light clicked on in the hallway. Footsteps. Katia appeared, looking agitated. Her blonde hair swayed as she shook her head. She tugged at clear plastic gloves on her wrists. At seeing me, she gasped.

Katia tried to outflank me. I planted my back against the doorknob. Our eyes met. I brandished the wrench.

Katia said, "I don't have to talk to you. I work here. You don't."

"You can talk to me, or you can talk to Stan." With my left hand, I slipped my phone out from a back pocket.

Katia, about five feet-two, sturdy, wore a long-sleeved black T-shirt, jeans and dark tennis shoes. Her hands were empty but for the clear gloves.

She said, "I'm leaving."

"We're going to talk."

I slid the phone into my jeans. I grabbed the back of a wood chair and slid it backwards, blocking the door. I set the wrench on the floor, and sat. "Why did you ask if I was Hal Bell?"

"I didn't."

"Sit. We have things to talk about."

Katia whispered, "Screw you," went to an armchair, and plopped onto it.

"I thought I heard you say 'Bell.' Maybe it was, 'hell'?"

She seized on that too quickly. "Yeah, I meant hell."

"That's one lie. Let's go to: what are you doing here?"

Anxiety kicked her Eastern European accent into high gear. "I just straightening up, after they leave."

"Why are you wearing gloves? And a long-sleeved shirt on a hot night?"

"I always want to be clean."

"I see. Do Stan and Laura know you're here, being clean?"

Her eyes dropped. Her gloved hands went to her belly, as if I'd provoked a stomachache. Katia pretended to be shy. "I thought to surprise them."

"You're a pretty good liar. I give you credit for that. Did you find any gold?"

Katia covered her eyes with gloved palms. She tried to make sobbing noises, but only produced a darkened look of sorrow. "My sister, Anna. She needs the green card. The lawyer, he's expensive."

"Why don't you ask Stan and Laura for the money? They could help you."

Katia manufactured the look of an innocent waif trying to help her sister. She swapped personas as effortlessly as flipping through a deck of playing cards. "I did. They say they pay enough. I should borrow, from bank. They say I should be thankful for the job."

Out came my phone. "That's easy enough to prove. I'll call Stan and ask him about it."

Katia jumped out of the chair. In the low light, her blue eyes shone like roadside flares. She thumped her right shoe against the wood floor. "Mr. Stan fire me if you call." She squeezed her fingers together at her belly button. "Don't tell. I didn't take nothing. Search me. You want to search me? You have nothing to prove."

I said, "I think you mean I can't prove anything."

"That, too!"

"Sit down. You may as well because I'm not letting you out this door until I'm ready to."

Katia's lower lip pushed forward in an emphatic pout. She sat in the chair, stared straight ahead, elbows on knees. "I don't talk because I didn't do anything."

"Okay. We won't talk. Empty your pockets, and you can go. Spend your vacation worrying about what I'll tell Stan and Laura when they get back."

"Go to hell, weird hand."

"It's possible," I said. "For now, empty your pockets, then go. Don't come back until the Whitneys return. Either that or I call Stan."

Katia emptied her left pocket. Nothing. She hesitated, gauging me, perhaps wondering what I'd do if she called my bluff and tried to force her way past me. I displayed the phone again. "How do you think I should explain all this to Stan?"

Reluctantly, Katia's right hand went into her jeans. She extracted a Ziploc baggie. She set it on the arm of the chair she'd sat in.

She said, "Now no reason to call Mr. Stan or Miss Laura."

"I'm not sure about that."

I stood, picked up the wrench, and shoved the wood chair to where it had been. I opened the front door. I held onto the top of its frame. "I hope you have a long night worrying about what I might do."

Katia dipped her head, said, "You go to hell," and walked into the purple night.

She passed the tennis court, the pool, and headed toward where Stan Whitney's SUV usually sat; it was at the airport parking lot. Soon as I thought Katia couldn't hear, I hustled around the other side of the tennis court, pool and house. Katia walked down the long lane of a driveway. I hadn't bothered to lock the gates; the Whitneys never did. Katia could have driven in. The pavement was smooth; I kept my steps light. Katia reached the public road. An engine started. The shadow of a vehicle appeared where the driveway reached Ralston Avenue. Katia stepped up at getting in. The vehicle's shadow seemed higher than a regular car, like a pickup truck. It pulled ahead. I headed back to the house. I heard another engine start. I glimpsed a passing pickup truck. It was large, and white.

I locked the black wrought iron gates. Somewhere down the street, an owl hooted, one, two, three times. Moments later, from a different direction, came a reply. I'd taken a dozen steps toward the house when I heard yet another vehicle's engine sound. I caught the passing shadow of a dark, tall and square vehicle, most likely a pickup truck. That was quite a parade of pickup trucks.

The night air was fresher out in McMansion Land than where I lived downtown. No gasoline smells in the warm summer night. No buzzing freeway sounds. A couple of parcels over, a rainbird soaked a lawn with a chug-chug-chug cadence that was nice but not as elegant as the owls exchanging calls again. While I found reasons to disparage the rich Whitneys, the truth was they'd built a wonderful place to live.

I returned to Clyde's old place, scooped up the Ziploc baggie, turned off the lights and locked the door. Before going to Karen's guesthouse, I went to the pool, stripped off my clothes and took a swim. I didn't know what to think about the pickup trucks. On the well-heeled streets of Crystal Meadows, pickup trucks usually belonged to hired help, gardeners, pool maintenance people, plumbers, someone who comes to power wash a driveway. At nine p.m., the odds of three pickups in a row passing by the Whitney residence were probably less than the odds that meeting Karen, via Clyde Whitney, was fate.

Sixteen

Friday afternoon, at the medical center, I became aware of a man watching me. At least I thought he watched me. In any large institution a few people lurk about who are off kilter. Also, during the previous six years, more than a few people couldn't keep their eyes off my sliced hand. It repulsed some; it fascinated others. The man who seemed to watch me looked to be in his late forties, give or take, six feet tall, of average build. Short brown hair was parted on the left. A thin white scar marked the base of his chin. Light of foot, he didn't strike me as a patient. He didn't seem an employee in that he appeared uncomfortable reading, or pretending to read, a glossy magazine while walking far behind me down a hallway. Like the small speedster I was unable to catch in the alley, this man didn't frighten me. Unlike the driver of the white pickup truck, this guy signaled no menace. In my years working for Sherman Investigations, I'd been wrong on that score twice. Neither had resulted in a happy ending.

Sunday, midday, I picked up Karen at Sacramento International Airport. Laura and Stan had decided to take advantage of being back East and spend time in New York. They had friends there, and Stan scheduled meetings with real estate investors.

Tired after a sunrise driving of a rental car to Logan International and then flying to Sacramento, with a two-hour layover in

116

Chicago, Karen let her body fall against mine during my welcome home hug. I put her suitcase on the Volvo's backseat. On the way to Crystal Meadows I kept squeezing her jeans at the knee.

Karen said, "I missed you. After a shower and some food, I'll show you how much."

"I'm just happy you're back."

Karen stretched her long narrow left arm around my neck. "It was a good trip, but exhausting. Other than Aunty Rae getting in a fight with my mom and Aunt Lila—she left in a huff on Wednesday—everybody was full of love." Karen opened and closed tired eyes. "Aunty Rae has it in her head Grandpa loved her like a daughter, not a niece. She's after money of course."

I said, "I hope you know how grateful I am to have known Clyde the little I did. He reminded me to think about what it means to be alive. If we have a purpose."

Karen said, "Damn you, Taylor." She wept softly the rest of the trip to Crystal Meadows.

We went into the guest house. Karen took a shower. Wrapped in a thick white towel, she came into the bedroom. She lay on the bed, eyes closed, on her back. Her damp hair smelled of lavender shampoo. I unwrapped the towel slowly, as if it were a bandage. Starting at her belly, I kissed my way up Karen's body, ending with kisses atop her fragrant scalp. I rolled her on her side, massaged her shoulders, slowly, gently. I massaged Karen until I felt her muscles let go. I moved her lovely hair aside and kissed the back of her neck.

I said, "How are you, Love?"

Karen answered with a light snore. I went to the kitchen and made a sandwich. I wondered about the trio of assumed pickup trucks that night, and the fellow observing me at the medical center.

*

Two hours later, we packed the Volvo. I'd shopped for Rattlesnake's provisions the day before. I drove. We passed orchards and horse ranches. Early August, the colors of most vegetation had diminished under the relentless sun of June and July.

Breaking a silent stretch, Karen said, "He had a good life."

"He had an astounding life."

Karen said, "Until Gram died, and he bought the mine and moved out here, we were all close. Except Uncle Stan, who went to UCLA and stayed in California. We'd go to their place outside Cambridge almost every weekend. Grandpa's favorite thing with the grandkids was elaborate treasure hunts. Maps led to more maps. Or you'd dig somewhere and find a box. In the box were words you had to put in a certain order to get the next clue."

We passed a reddish barn with the ranch's cattle brand painted in whitewash above the barn's main door.

Karen said, "Even as a kid, you knew he was special."

We reached the levee road, Garden Highway. To the left flowed the broad Sacramento River.

I said, "Are you comfortable discussing the case?"

"Can't we just be happy for a while?"

I described the man following me in the med center.

"It could be anything. You've been paranoid since that guy ran you off the road."

"True."

I told Karen about finding Katia in the guesthouse, and catching her with a baggy of gold dust. I recounted our exchanges. I told Karen about following Katia down the driveway to Ralston Avenue, and the three what I assumed were pickup trucks.

Karen snorted. "I knew we couldn't trust her." She pursed her

118

lips. Then came the Whitney frown. "I don't like the three pickups. That's worse. No way it's coincidental."

"Exactly."

"Why didn't you call me?"

"I didn't want to upset anyone while you were involved in something more meaningful. Second, I wanted to wait till you and I talked it over. We might be able to use not telling Stan and Laura about Katia's stealing to our advantage. Give her funny looks when we see her. Keep her worried."

Karen pulled her ponytail around. She brushed it across her lips. "Go on."

"I'm sure she said Bell's name when I came in. When I get her alone, I'll ask if she wants to talk to me, or Stan about it. Give her a time frame to choose."

"What if she lies to you?"

"She'll lie. It still might lead to something."

Karen gave my upper arm one of her buddy punches. "You're not going to let go of this, are you?"

"Not until I'm satisfied I know what happened with Clyde."

We crossed the bridge where the Feather River joined the Sacramento. I checked the rearview mirror for pickup trucks. I turned right at the first road. Karen got out and unlocked the gate. We drove past drained rice paddies. Blackbirds reeled overhead. The flat landscape, kept in check by the rice growers, was treeless until we crossed the bridge that took us onto Genoa Island.

Like the first time we arrived, the goat called Henry Ford ambled onto the road. I cut the Volvo's engine. Karen and I climbed out. Rattlesnake Johnson stormed from the cabin, Winchester rifle in hand. He raised it to a shoulder and pointed it toward Karen and me. Gray hair wild, milky eyes the same, Rattlesnake shouted, "I heard the car! I know where to shoot."

His parched voice ratcheted higher. "Damn you, who's there? You speak up or I shoot!"

Henry Ford ran away, kicking back dust. Karen and I put our hands up in reflexive responses, even though Rattlesnake couldn't see them.

Karen called ahead: "It's Karen. We're here with supplies."

Rattlesnake bent at the knees. He fanned the rifle left and right, lifted his bony, sun-scorched nose.

Karen said, "Don't you recognize my voice?""

He gazed around blankly, took a big sniff of air. Satisfied, he set the rifle on the picnic table. He said, "I'm right sorry about Clyde. I'd been missing him, ever since he couldn't come here anymore. But last time we were together, he told me he was ready to go. He said he'll make it back to Joanie."

Our hands dropped.

"Rattlesnake, it's Jeff. We will help you in any way we can."

He said, "It's Jeff? Really? Why, I was expecting the governor. Why do you think I'm so dumb?"

"Sorry. Did Hal Bell come out and tell you about Clyde?"

"Didn't need to. You all come aboard. I'll tell you about it. And something else that ain't no damn good."

We brought the grocery bags to the cabin doorway. Rattlesnake conveyed them inside. The yellow tabby cat appeared, jumped onto the table and landed inches from the rifle's trigger. That provoked a cringe from me. I moved the rifle to where I'd last seen it, leaning against the side of the cabin, left of the doorway.

Rattlesnake brought out a jug of water. Before setting it down, he said, "Could you put that rifle next to the door for me?"

I went through the motions of taking the Winchester, hitting a knuckle on the table and then against the cabin wall by the door. Rattlesnake's face looked like something wasn't quite right as he shushed the cat off the table. Karen arranged the squeaky wooden chairs while Rattlesnake brought water glasses, chunks of beef jerky on a paper plate, and three of those dirty cloth napkins we'd used before.

Rattlesnake scratched a circle in his gray beard's nest. He took a piece of jerky and tore off a strip with his teeth. He said, "I like to sit out here and listen to the shortwave. I get this station from Topeka, where they run through the mercantile exchange on the hour. Soybeans, beef cattle, cotton, oil, natural gas, you name it. It reminds me of my dad. That's what he listened to."

I tore off a strip of beef jerky. Henry Ford appeared. He clambered up the two wood steps, found shade near the cabin wall, and plunked onto the deck. The island's songbirds played their symphony. I understood why an independent man like Rattlesnake chose to live out there alone. In its own pale and peaceful way, it was a paradise.

Rattlesnake waved his right arm overhead, as if to add emphasis. "I'm listening to beef cattle prices come so fast I can't hardly follow. Next thing I know, the sounds get scratchy. I play with the dial. Out come gurgling sounds. It's like the radio is underwater. It keeps up the gurgling till I'm shaking all over, and don't know why. The sounds stop. Without thinking about it, I say 'God bless you, brother Clyde.' The words just come out. I knew he was gone. Go ahead and think I'm crazy. That don't bug me none."

Karen said, "I believe you."

I said, "Anything is possible with Clyde Whitney."

Rattlesnake looked off to places I couldn't guess at. We chewed jerky. A gentle wind fluttered through the oak and digger pines.

Rattlesnake's eyes opened wide. "Jesus Christ, am I slippin'. I near forgot what's made me so jumpy I practically shot you."

Karen said, "As Grandpa used to say, 'Everything's okay, we just keep forgetting.'"

Rattlesnake said, "That is a fact. He'd say that whenever I'd get riled over something going wrong. Here is another fact. Two days ago, I'm taking a rest on the cot. I don't hear a car, but I hear what I know are people steps. I go to get the Winchester. It's gone. Some little feller says, 'Have a seat at the table. You just sit there. I'm going to take a look around.' He was very polite about it. Formal like."

Rattlesnake scratched at his beard, gave it a tug.

I said, "How much can you see? Sometimes I think you see more than you let on."

"I see some shadows. They float, kind of like ghosts."

I said, "The first time I came here, you were thirty feet away and referred to me as tall. Now you say this guy was little. You must see more than you let on."

Rattlesnake giggled. He turned to Karen. "This boyfriend of yours, he always underestimates me." Rattlesnake stood. "When you can't see, your ears become your eyes. Your nose, too. When someone talks at me, I'm aware of where it comes from. Like this."

Rattlesnake's forefinger tapped his forehead in a salute. "This is me." He lowered the leveled hand two inches. "Karen." The hand rose to about four inches above his head. "Jeff." Next, his hand dropped to well below the gray beard. "Here is the little feller."

Clearly satisfied with himself, Rattlesnake sat so smoothly the rickety chair didn't squeak.

Karen said, "Did he say anything else?"

"He just kept saying 'Please stay seated.' Since he had the Winchester, I didn't push matters."

I said, "Where'd he look?"

"Inside the cabin first. Poked through everything. Then around the sheds. I know the wood sounds. He fought the door to Hotel Tin but couldn't get it open. He pressured me for keys. I told him I don't have any. I say, 'what good would keys do a blind man?

They don't give me no keys.'" Rattlesnake added, "I got 'em where nobody will ever find them."

Rattlesnake looked up, like he was trying to recall something. "Funny thing was, I didn't hear no car. Car sounds carry loud out here."

Karen said, "What if you were sleeping?

Rattlesnake said, "I'm ninety-five percent sure I'd have heard a vehicle. Later, I walk to the gate. You can't climb over, on account of the way the barbed wire goes out. No holes were cut in the gate. I say he came by boat, in the canal. It happens off and on."

Karen and I peppered Rattlesnake with questions. Did the man have an accent? Did he seem to know you were here, or did he seem surprised you were here? Was there any indication someone else was with him?

Every answer was no.

Rattlesnake said, "I have a question for you two. Why don't I get you some keys?"

He went into the cabin. Karen and I stood, stretched, and hugged.

She said, "What do you think it means, this guy showing up here?"

"It means I'm going to get paranoid again."

Rattlesnake came outside holding a key in each gaunt hand. He shook one. "You remember this from Hotel Tin. The other opens the storage sheds." He smiled. For the first time, I noticed he had a full set of teeth. His gaze was direct, honest. It made sense he and Clyde had gotten on so well.

Rattlesnake said, "Go ahead, make us rich."

I looked to Karen.

She said, "I thought about it when I was back home, watching Uncle Stan take over everything. He kept reminding us he's executor of the estate. To hell with that. Let's go for it."

Karen said she'd stay and chat with Rattlesnake. I took a flashlight from Karen's car and went to the tin, warehouse-like structure. For light I pushed open the grinding door as far as I could. Inside, the smell of long-settled water mixed with the scent of wet soil. This time: no adrenaline rush. A peacefulness came over me as I resumed the hunt for Ziploc baggies half filled with gold dust. I felt no urgency. I pictured Clyde wandering through the open space, lights on, pockets filled with offerings for when his time came. He'd get confused. He'd drop a baggy and forget all about it. A great mind going to pot.

I left Hotel Tin with three baggies. Karen was on the porch alone. The door to the cabin was shut. Rattlesnake had gone inside to take his siesta. I sat across from Karen at the picnic table.

I said, "We tell Rattlesnake about these, right?"

Karen blew aside strands of hair trailing over her eyes. "Any we find, he gets a share."

I pulled a key out of a front pocket. "Let's see what's in the sheds."

We found three more. A tremendous return for two hours' effort. My thoughts circled back to finding enough gold to pay my medical school debts.

Karen knocked on the cabin door.

Rattlesnake said, "Who's there?"

Karen said, "What?"

Behind the door, he snickered. "I'm joking." He opened the door and stepped onto the porch.

Karen said, "We found six little baggies of gold dust. We consider part of it yours. We'll be back Sunday after next."

"Get us rich before your uncle gives me the boot."

Karen said, "You sure you're okay out here? You're welcome to come stay in Crystal Meadows for a few days."

Rattlesnake shook his head. He made a *phooey* sound. "And not do my job as head of security?"

I drove the dusty road to the canal. I entered the gate code. It crawled open, screeching, ancient sounding. I pressed the gas pedal, rattled across the steel bridge—and slammed on the brakes before running over what I thought was a long snake stretched perpendicular to the road. It didn't move. I observed two-inch barbs rising from a spike strip, the kind police lay across traffic lanes to puncture the tires of a fleeing suspect. I bounced out of the car. Karen joined me.

I pointed to the strip of upturned metal barbs. "Somebody's still trying to scare us off."

I stalked around to the back of Karen's Volvo. I lay on the ground, pushed myself under the bumper. I saw a rectangular device clamped to the frame. I laughed so hard I banged my forehead on the underside of the car. I let the back of my head rest on baked earth and laughed some more.

Karen walked to behind the back bumper. "Hey Taylor. What's so funny?"

It took a few coughs to tamp down the chuckling. "Everything's funny. Life, liberty, the pursuit of happiness." I couldn't stop more laughter from bubbling forth. "Somebody planted a tracking device on you. A Vehicle Tracker 180. That's how he knew we're here."

I got out from under the car. I went into the trunk for Karen's toolbox. Two minutes later I had the Vehicle Tracker in hand. I disabled it. I rolled up the spike strip, put it and the Vehicle Tracker in the trunk.

I said, "I'm sure there will be one under the Jetta. I'll throw it in the garbage. Let them figure out why it's making the rounds of city streets."

I drove past the drained rice paddies. Every couple of minutes I broke into soft laughter.

Karen said, "I get the impression you're having fun."

"More and more all the time."

"What's fun about someone beating you up, someone else robbing your house, and now we're threatened?"

"It reminds me I'm alive?"

"Just don't," Karen said. Her voice trailed off. She took in a lot of air before saying, "You know, just don't go after this so hard we end up getting killed."

The thought had never occurred to me. It ended conversation. Karen unlocked the combination locks at the gate. That they weren't snapped off made me think the person who planted the spike strip arrived by water, as Rattlesnake theorized about who we nicknamed The Little Feller. But how did he get on the other side of the fence?

We headed south on Garden Highway, the Sacramento River to the right, orchards and ranches below and left. Not stunning country, not Yosemite or Lake Tahoe, yet beautiful in a bucolic, old days sort of way. Tires hummed on asphalt.

Karen finally said, "The reason I blew up at you that time is partly history, partly fear."

"Okay."

"When you grow up with money in your family, people become your friend for the wrong reason. Especially guys."

"Did your ex rip you off for money, like your dad with your mom?"

"He didn't succeed. And I'd like to modify a quote by someone we both know. Your field is pediatrics, not psychiatry."

"Fair enough."

Karen said, "I came here to nursing school to wipe the slate clean. Move on from my ex."

"Does this ex have a name?"

"Rick. Rick Anthor. Why does it matter?"

"I want to think of him as a person, no matter how bad a guy he is."

"Fine. Three weeks of a clean-slate life, nothing on my mind except learning how to help people instead of making money doing coding for a company called AppAnswers. Three weeks. Then I meet you and everything's bonkers." Karen pulled her chestnut ponytail around and nibbled at it. She looked to her knees. "I'm too crazy about you for my own good. I mean, here I am joining you in going after Grandpa's gold, for God's sake. It isn't only that I don't want Uncle Stan or Hal Bell to steal it. I'm doing it because I'm batty about you. I want to do crazy things with you."

"So, in a way, you are having fun."

Karen shook her head, looked outside. "You truly are impossible."

Seventeen

Tuesday morning, Karen drove to class. I lounged around the Whitney compound, living the life of a country squire. I checked the price of gold. I wondered if we could sell the gold to someone under the table, make it tax free.

My phone pinged. It showed a name rather than numbers.

"Mr. Bell," I said. "It's been a while."

"It sure has." His voice, forceful, rose. "I would've thought you'd call to let me know about Clyde. What a sad ending to a good life."

"Sorry. I assumed Katia told you."

Silence. Then: "Why would you think that?"

"The first time I came to 3134 Ralston Avenue, the two of you were arguing along the side of the house. You came around the corner and were surprised to see me. You two seemed to know each other well."

"I don't recall that."

"It doesn't matter. And I have been remiss in checking in with you. With Stan back East—he and Laura are staying on in New York—his car's just sitting at the airport."

Bell cleared his throat. "I got to say, I was offended when I asked Stan about a funeral, and he tells me it's family only. Hell, I spent more time with Clyde than that spoiled son of his ever did."

"I'm glad you called. Stan hasn't demonstrated an inkling of meeting anyone who might have put that tracker on you. He just goes to work, has business lunches, goes home. With Clyde gone, I propose we drop the matter."

"What kind of damage do you think you're entitled to, dollars wise?"

"I didn't find anything. How about if I keep the CarScout, though I don't know what for, and we call it even."

"I don't have to worry about you telling Stan, or Karen? I don't have to give you money to keep you quiet? That makes for tricky believing."

"You think I want Karen to know I was going to take money to keep track of her uncle? No way."

Bell's temperature cooled. "Okay. It never happened. I guess not much really did."

I said, "That is correct."

Bell said, "Who do you guess put that thing on my truck? It sure as hell didn't get there by itself."

"One candidate is Katia. From what I hear, she's been nosy about Clyde. Which reminds me. Did Katia mention running into me the other night? While in Clyde's guesthouse?"

Bell said, "I have no idea what you're talking about."

"Maybe I don't, either. You take care now."

I clicked off. I wondered how long before Bell relayed our conversation to Katia. If Katia hadn't told him about being caught in the guesthouse, so much the better. It might set them at odds with each other, as might me suggesting Katia could be the person behind having Bell's pickup tracked. When people argue, sometimes they want to complain about it to a third party.

I got ready for a morning run. I stepped outside of the guesthouse and headed for the street. Poking above the top line of stucco wall in lieu of a property line fence was the white roof of a pickup truck.

I heard a door shut. I hurried back inside. I went to a zippered pocket in my suitcase. I grabbed the thirty-eight Smith & Wesson I'd checked out at Sherman Investigations and removed from my car before dropping it at the garage. I'd thought it unwise to leave a loaded gun at my place for a week.

I scooted around a corner of the guesthouse. I heard steps on the cement walkway. No way was I going to let this guy kick the crap out of me again. I continued around the guesthouse, counterclockwise, and ended up a dozen feet behind a pair of broad shoulders stretching a short sleeved brown shirt. The man's short hair was the same brown as his shirt. He approached the guesthouse door. A hand reached into the front right pocket of jeans.

I said, "Both hands up. You run, I'll shoot you in the ass."

The man stopped walking.

I said, "Hands all the way up. Walk slowly, to the pool. Come on. Walk over to the pool."

"How do I know you got a weapon? You don't seem the type."

I turned toward the deep end of the swimming pool and blew a hole in blue water. The man recoiled.

"Keep your hands high. Walk. Go to the pool." He crossed from the concrete path onto the apron of the pool. He halted. I remained a dozen feet back. "Walk down the steps, into the water."

"Hey, man. You're taking this too far."

"Walk to where the water's just below your chin. As in right now."

"What the hell is this all about?"

"It's all about you. You've followed me at least twice. You stomped me. Now you're a prowler with a history of assaulting me. I might have to shoot you in self-defense."

My mind churned a hundred miles per hour. I worried a

neighbor might report hearing a gunshot. If the police came, I'd tell them everything straight up. A decree grilled into me at Sherman Investigations: never lie to the police. It almost always catches up to you.

"Keep going. To your chin, center of the pool. Don't test me. I hear being shot hurts like hell."

The man shook his head. He trudged down the pool's steps into water. He advanced to where the water was just beneath his chin. I steadied the gun with both hands, aimed at below the back of his neck.

"Turn around. Keep your hands up."

The man turned around. His eyes were green, intense and gleaming with a familiar menace. I'd seen similar gleaming eyes working for Sherman Investigations. They meant inevitable combat. Below this guy's eyes, brown stubble grew in uneven patches. His left ear was thickened from too many blows, his nose askew from probably the same. I guessed his age as thirty-five, forty at most.

I said, "Put your face in the water. Drink some."

"You're crazy."

"Crazy enough to shoot you. Now put your face underwater, and drink some."

"No way."

I blew another hole in pool water. He tripped, found his footing.

"Put your face under and drink."

"You're a crazy son of a bitch."

I waved the pistol at him. He did as told. He came up coughing.

I said, "Drowning would be a terrible way to die. Don't you think? Did you drown Clyde Whitney?"

"I never met Clyde Whitney."

"I got four left. It only takes one."

The man coughed and spat water. He managed, "Look, man. We can talk this through."

"I talk, you answer. Did you break into Clyde Whitney's house in Pine Grove?"

"I never broke into anybody's house."

"Yet you're here. Like a burglar. I've got a right to defend myself. Or you could tell me what you're doing here."

Wide eyes on the gun, he shook his head.

"If you don't talk, you'll spend the whole day standing in the pool, wondering if I'll shoot if you climb out. I will."

Sweat rolled down his forehead. He blinked at it.

I kept the pistol on him and walked around the pool. He turned a quarter circle, watching me. I bent over and flipped open a mini refrigerator tucked under one of the glass tables, scooped out a plastic bottle of mineral water. Keeping hold of the pistol with my left hand, I flung the bottle at him with my bad right hand. He caught it.

"Drink up. Looks like it's going to be a long day."

The man unscrewed the cap, sipped water. I sat in a poolside chair, used both hands to steady the thirty-eight again. Still no siren.

Eyes on the gun, the man said, "Your car's not here. That's supposed to mean you're not around."

"I happen to be staying here." I stood, extended the gun in his direction. "What's the reason for your visit?"

"It's just a job, man. You can put that thing down."

"Tell me about the job, man."

He shrugged, making a slight wave in the pool. "Stan Whitney's a pompous ass. Why risk mine for him?"

"Now we're making progress. Keep talking. I wouldn't want this to go off because I got impatient."

The man drank mineral water. He squirmed in five feet of beautiful swimming pool water. "A guy I do work for sometimes, he referred me to Whitney. Stan says you're a gold digger. He says you're chasing his niece when she's vulnerable, after a divorce. Stan wants you to go away."

"Take it from the top. What have you done for him?"

"Well, first he had me follow this mining buddy of old Mr. Whitney's, who Stan said was after his father's gold. I called Stan about you following the same guy. Soon as I mentioned your hand—I seen you in my binocs walking by the river—Stan told me who you are, how you're hustling his niece. He told me to switch over to you, make you nervous about getting involved with her. See if I could get rid of you."

"Did he tell you to stomp me?"

An arrogant smile. "That was my idea. Whitney's got a shit load of money. I figured if I got rid of you pronto, he'd shell out big time. So I knocked you around. When you kept coming for the niece, I followed you some more." The man was on a roll. "Put that spike strip out by the island. I'm glad I blew up your tires."

"You didn't. I saw it. Did you come in by boat?"

"By boat? Of course not. I watched you with binoculars go to the bridge. After you and Whitney's niece went on the island, and the gate shut, I drove in and unrolled the spike strip. Why the hell would I need a boat?"

"But the locks to the road to the rice paddies weren't snapped."

"You don't need to bust them when you got the combinations."

"Stan?"

He nodded.

I waved the pistol at him. "What about the tracking devices?"

"What tracking devices?"

"The one under Karen's car, and mine."

He looked confused. "Whatever you're talking about, they didn't come from me. I just followed you from a distance."

I wouldn't have believed him except he'd offered the other information readily. So, I wasn't sure about the trackers.

I said, "Let's get back to why you're a prowler, and I have to defend myself."

"I'm supposed to search the guesthouses. See if you have any gold. Stan thinks you're out scouting for gold his dad is supposed to have socked away. Just like that Bell. He thinks you may have pulled his niece into it."

"Does Stan pay well? He should, considering what he's asking."

A second arrogant smile. "In hundreds. Neat little stacks. They come in the mail." His right arm dropped. The man said, "I got the guesthouse keys in my pocket. Should I show you?"

"Keep your hands up."

I took the gun with my left hand. I slipped my phone out of my jeans with my right. "Say cheese." I clicked photos. "Here's how it's going to be. I won't email these embarrassing pictures of you in the pool fully dressed to Stan. I won't tell anybody about our conversation. I won't report you to the police. On your end, you tell Stan you searched the guesthouses. You found nothing unusual. Then beg off. Tell him I've caught onto you following me."

"What's in it for you to keep it a secret? What do you get?"

"Maybe I'm a gold digger. Now that we understand each other, it's time for you to move on."

I shooed him to the pool steps with the pistol. He climbed out, dripping globs of water. His tennis shoes made squishing sounds on the poolside cement. His sopping wet jeans shined under sunlight.

Neither of us spoke as I followed him down the concrete path along the side of the big house, and down the long driveway. His clothes hung heavy and tight on him. His footsteps left dark prints. At the gate he took out a key, unlocked the gate and swung it inward. We walked onto Ralston Avenue. The large white Ram pickup was twenty yards to the right.

Before he reached it, I said, "Stop."

He sighed, and halted. "Fuck you."

"Take out your wallet. You can keep everything but the driver's license. Slide it out, drop it on the ground. Then get lost."

"Fuck you."

My hand jumped as the thirty-eight blasted a bullet through the raised tailgate of the pickup, leaving a clean hole there and who knew where else.

The man froze.

I said, "Three down, three to go. The next one goes in your leg."

His right hand reached back, found the wallet. He opened it. He removed his license from of its slot and dropped it on asphalt.

I said, "My word's good. Nothing to Stan, nothing to the police. You get clear of Stan. You made good money, and you don't get shot. If I ever see you again, I'll shoot your dick off."

The man walked to the driver's door of the pickup. His shoes squished and left footprints. He climbed in and drove off. His parting shot was to thrust his left arm out of the window and flip me the bird.

I picked up the driver's license. His name: Dennis McKay. The letters appeared wavy. When I walked, my balance was off. I locked the black wrought-iron gates behind me, walked up the driveway. Once inside the guesthouse, I went to the bedroom where my suitcase lay open on the bed. I removed the three remaining bullets from the Smith & Wesson, put them and the gun in the compartment where I'd hidden it. I zipped the compartment closed. I went into the bathroom, knelt on the tile floor and dry heaved over the bathtub.

Eighteen

Via an internet search, I learned Dennis McKay's cell number, and that he owned the property in Folsom listed on his driver's license. Nothing more. He lived in a nice neighborhood even though he had no employment history I could find. McKay did not possess a license to operate as a private investigator. That Stan Whitney knew how to get in touch with a guy like Dennis McKay told me Stan's business affairs probably weren't always as tidy as his crisp white shirts implied.

Back from school, Karen looked over McKay's driver's license, dropped it on the coffee table. In the middle of the day, I'd remembered to fish the spent bullets from the swimming pool. I told Karen everything.

Her cheeks blazed. "What do you expect me to say? You did good? It's okay for you to fire a gun? A *gun*, Jeff? I get it you were scared. That doesn't justify what you did."

"I don't think he'll be back. It was crazy, but he wasn't going to disappear. And by the way, I don't appreciate your uncle hiring a tough guy to follow me around and rough me up."

"Neither do I. But it doesn't change a thing."

I said, "Tomorrow morning, I'm returning the pistol to Clint. I'm not acting rational. I'm too wrapped up in this to keep my head on straight."

Karen said, "It's one thing after another with you."

She went to the kitchen. I heard the refrigerator door open. Karen returned holding a bottle of beer. She broke into giddy laughter that expressed uncertainty. "You really did that? You shot two bullets into the pool?"

"And one in his truck."

Karen lifted the beer bottle, swallowed. "Taylor, you're a stubborn mule."

Karen went outside. I watched her cross the concrete walkway and sit at one of the glass tables with a fake kerosene lantern at its center. The lonely, insecure boy I'd been growing up percolated through me, spreading fear of abandonment into my heart. Karen seemed to not look at anything. She set down the bottle of beer.

I took a beer from the refrigerator, uncapped it and joined Karen at the glass table. The translucent blue pool water shimmered under sunlight. In that moment, it did not seem inviting.

Karen said, "You know what else bothers me about you?"

"Go ahead. Make a list."

"You understood Grandpa better than me. I can tell, by the things you say about him. You tried to get in sync with Grandpa's thinking in ways I never did."

"I didn't need to try. He drew me in by who he was."

Karen said, "I don't know where you came from. I don't know where I came from. Sometimes I don't think anybody really knows anything."

"Clyde knew things. He knew the important things. If somebody harmed him, I'm going to make him pay."

The next morning, Karen drove us to my place, dropped me off, then drove to the medical center. I called Dr. Fisher. I said something had happened that meant I was going to be a couple of hours late.

Dr. Fisher said, "Being a medical doctor requires a certain level of consistency. Level-headedness and consistency."

"I know I'm failing."

"You're not failing with the patients. You're good with patients. You're failing with yourself."

I didn't argue the point.

I walked to the Sherman Investigations office carrying the pistol in a brown grocery bag, along with three unspent bullets. From there I'd go pick up my car at the garage. I'd been tardy in taking care of that, too. The truth: I was a tangle of half thoughts, worries, fantasies, schemes. Clint wasn't in. I set the brown bag on the reception counter.

Natalie gave me a questioning look. I said goodbye and left the office. I couldn't get my thoughts in order.

I walked east, up the numbered streets of the Capitol District. I forgot all about the car. Golden squirrels rustled about. The warm morning promised another hundred-degree day. I came to an urban park. Two men and a woman shot baskets. I envied their playfulness. Chills pulsated down my back. I turned around and there he was, the man from the medical center. This time he wasn't hiding behind a copy of *Sports Illustrated.* I had more important things on my mind than dealing with being followed again. I was going to get in this man's face big time, sans weapon.

I headed across the park's lawn. At the other end of the grass sat twin bathrooms of pinkish concrete. I went into the men's room, counted to fifteen, burst out and ran straight at the man, who stood in the middle of the grass. I expected a chase or a fight. The man stood with arms to his sides, a numb look on his face.

His short brown hair was thinning and flecked with gray. His eyes were hazel, and sad looking. He looked fit. Clean shaven, his blue shirt tucked into gray cords that ended at gray tennis shoes.

He was nervous. You saw it in his face.

I went right up to him. "Why are you following me?"

He spoke in a low, flat tone. "It's not that I'm following you."

I grabbed the front of his shirt and yanked it left and right, ripping it from his cords. I shoved him backwards. "If you're not following me, what do you call it?"

His light eyes flickered. He stepped back, glanced to the ground. "I'd like to think I'm looking out for you."

"No weird crap today. I'm done with it." I shoved him back two more steps. "Tell me who you're working for or I'm going to hurt you."

He turned sideways, still gazing downward. Again in a low register: "My name's Greg Naugle." He scuffed a tennis shoe on the grass. "I live in Stockton." He shook his head. "I don't know what to say. Maybe you can think of me kind of like an uncle."

He was too forlorn looking to smack. "How in the hell could you be my uncle?"

He walked a half circle. He stopped, looked off toward the basketball court. The ball made bouncing sounds. A guy took a shot; it clanged off the rim. The man who said he was from Stockton kept his gaze away from me.

He said, "I'm your father."

"What's the game? Does it have anything to do with Stan Whitney's games? Are you working for him, trying to screw with my head?"

Greg Naugle faced me. He sank to the grass. "I don't have any excuses. I'm your father, but I've never been a dad to you."

The words hit me like an axe to the gut. I, too, sank to the grass. A swarm of black dots stopped me from seeing plainly.

I said, "Why now? Why not twenty or twenty-five years ago?"

I looked at him. He didn't look at me.

He talked to the grass. "I was nineteen. Your mom and I had been going out less than a year. Neither of us was close to ready to get married. When she packed up her Datsun, and moved way up north, everybody knew why. I ran off to San Diego. Took classes at the junior college."

I said, "I don't know if I want to talk to you. Actually, I don't."

Red-rimmed eyes searched mine. Naugle said, "I don't blame you. Not at all. But I must tell you, you're being followed by two men."

"I know. I think I got rid of one yesterday."

"The one with the muscles, or the one in the Honda Accord?"

"The one with the big white pickup."

Naugle said, "Good. He looks dangerous."

"Wait a second. How do you know I'm being followed?"

Greg Naugle lifted his untucked shirt and wiped his face with it. "I parked down the block from your house, trying to work up the guts to knock on the door. I rehearsed excuses for not coming through for you." He wiped his nose, cleared his throat. "A guy drives to in front of your place, gets out and clicks pictures with his phone. This is the one with the muscles. He looks around, goes back to the truck and drives away."

"So, that was you following the pickup. I saw you make a U-turn."

"How? Your house was dark."

"It doesn't matter. What about the other one?"

"The next night, I do the same. I chicken out again. I'm sitting there when a Honda Accord pulls up. Because of the night before, I watch close. The guy gets out. He moves like a cat. He's under your car doing something I can't see. He gets back in his car. I duck as he drives on, then make a U-turn and follow him. I don't know if this helps, but he has a Nevada license plate."

"It confirms a suspicion."

Naugle said, "He makes a right, then a quick right and drives down the alley. I didn't follow him. It would've been too obvious. After that I started keeping watch on your place. I started going to the university medical center. I saw the one with the muscles there once in the parking lot. The other, twice."

He wiped his face, and got to his feet. I stood.

He said, "Why are they following you?"

I shook my head, indicating I wasn't going to tell him. I said, "I can't deal with this. I'm going."

He plucked a card from his wallet, offered it. I shook my head again. He offered the card a second time, then dropped it on the grass.

I said, "Why can't you just leave me alone?"

Head down, Greg Naugle stepped toward the basketball court. He stopped. He turned around. "Because I have cancer. We don't know how it's going to go. I had to see you at least once, to tell you I know I wronged you."

He walked away. He let out an anguished wail that interrupted the basketball players, who stared at him as he passed by. I watched until he disappeared around the corner of the next block.

I picked up the card.

GREG L. NAUGLE, CAPTAIN
FIRE DEPARTMENT, CITY OF STOCKTON
STATION #8

In the lower left corner was a telephone number and a City of Stockton email address.

I walked. I forgot about picking up the car. Passing a parked one, I came out of a fog, retrieved the old blue Jetta and drove

SCOTT LIPANOVICH

home. I Googled the Stockton Fire Department. Captain Naugle grew up in Atwater, same as my mom, and joined the force twenty-two years earlier. He'd won a bravery medal, another for community service. The last paragraph of the brief biography read: "Captain Naugle and his wife, Maureen, live in Stockton. Maureen is principal at Stanton Elementary School. They are proud parents of a daughter in college and a son in high school."

Another shock. I had a half-sister and a half-brother, and a stepmom. I went outside and walked some more. I'd spent my childhood obsessed with wondering who my father was. My mom had adroitly avoided talking about him. Then, completely without warning, he shows up when I'm twenty-eight and life is complicated. And he has cancer.

Almost unaware I was doing it, I slid my phone out and tapped it. At getting Karen's voicemail, I said, "The man shadowing me at the med center, it turns out he's my dad. I'm coming unglued. I don't know what to think. I don't know what to do."

142

Nineteen

Sprawled on the couch in the living room, head buried on Karen's heart, my arms encircled her. Karen's scent supplied a stream of comfort. If she hadn't come into my life, I don't think I could have handled meeting Greg Naugle.

I said, "It's too late. I don't want to see him." Five seconds later, I said, "I want to do the right thing, but I don't know what the right thing is."

Karen said, "There's no hurry. You're in shock. Your eyes are almost blank. Your voice is different."

Karen rocked us. "Give yourself a couple of days. Call him, see what it's like. You don't have to become buddies. You don't have to do anything. Still, you should call him because he's sick, and he reached out."

My mind spun, remembering how badly I'd wanted to be like the other kids in school and have a dad, even if their parents were divorced.

Karen said, "The way he checked out you being followed, it shows he cares."

"We got enough going on. It's too late."

"By the way, did you get rid of the gun this morning, like you said you would?"

"Of course."

"Good. If the answer were no, I'd have to leave."

Karen returned to school. I recorded the information on McKay's driver's license, folded a sheet of notebook paper around it, put it in a stamped envelope and clipped it to my box as outgoing mail. I called Burt's Boats, a rental and repair yard across the river, in West Sacramento. I arranged to have use of a fourteen-foot skiff.

Burt Monsen and I had a history. While working for Clint Sherman, I'd rented everything from a speedboat to a salmon trawler to a houseboat from him. The speedboat was for surveilling a city council member's teenage son. She suspected him of night running methamphetamine from Red Bluff, far up the Sacramento River, back downriver to an almond storage warehouse in nearby Clarksburg. She'd overhead part of a phone conversation. I'd caught the boy, confiscated the drugs and threatened him on behalf of a drug-running gang whose existence I made up on the fly.

The houseboat rental was a more nuanced assignment. I was to take two men into the dozens of interconnected sloughs of the Sacramento-San Joaquin Delta. Clint said the men needed a little down time. He instructed me not to inquire about their line of business; I'd receive a stout bonus. Their pale, puffy cheeks revealed them as indoor folk. At meals handguns sat immediately to the right of their plates. Second night out, about ten p.m., a boat slowly cruised by, displaying minimal lights for such a dark hour. Both men squatted on the deck, pistols drawn. I lay flat on the floor of the elevated steering cabin. None of us changed positions. At daybreak, a voice from below announced, "That wasn't the Albanese brothers. They'd have come back for us. Let's have gimpy fix us a drink."

At the end of our phone conversation, Burt expressed surprise at me reciting a credit card number, rather than showing up with an envelope containing greenbacks from Clint Sherman's safe.

"I'm in medical school now."

Burt said, "No need to pretend with me."

"I'll call ahead. I'm thinking Saturday morning at ten."

I said goodbye and headed to the kitchen for something to eat. My phone made the familiar sounds. I saw Clint's name, and tapped.

"Hello."

"Hello yourself. Natalie gets a grocery bag with the thirty-eight, and three bullets are missing from the chamber? You walk out, no explanation. You know you're supposed to document every shot. I don't care if it's a tin can."

"That sounds worse than it is."

"Are you in trouble?"

"Clint, if it was real trouble, I'd tell you."

"I don't like not knowing about the three empties. And you left without signing in the firearm."

"A few things are hitting me at once. I didn't even think about signing."

"Natalie says you don't look right."

"I'm not right. I have a lot on my mind. You got a minute? I mean several minutes."

I told Clint about the encounter with Dennis McKay, forcing him into the pool and to drink water. This brought an appreciative laugh.

"He might come back, but you did good. You can't stay passive with these people. It only eggs them on."

I told Clint about walking to pick up my car after dropping off the gun, and being followed. I said I'd previously seen this man following me at the medical center. "Long and short, he's my father. After all these years, he just shows up and introduces himself."

Clint said, "I thought you didn't have a dad, so to speak."

"I still don't, in any real sense."

"How were matters left?"

"He has cancer. He said they don't know how it's going to turn out. He wanted to apologize for not coming around when I was growing up."

Clint said, "It was probably the best he could do, considering the history."

"You want the truth? I'm more interested in finding out what happened with Clyde Whitney than in getting to know a Stockton fireman."

Clint said, "Your plate is full. Be careful with the Clyde Whitney portion. There are a lot of loose ends. It could still be risky. Call me any time."

I didn't make it to the medical center until almost three o'clock. Dr. Fisher looked up as I entered his office, looked down and continued typing on his computer. I wished him a good afternoon. He nodded. The afternoon played out with me doing the initial physical exams and then him following up. Dr. Fisher stayed in neutral.

At day's end, putting his white lab coat on its hanger, his back to me, Dr. Fisher said, "See you on Friday."

"See you on Friday." *TELEGRAPHING (twice!)*

Karen stopped by for dinner. She'd come immediately when, desperate, I'd left that voice message. Now that things were settling down, there was a subtle awkwardness. I figured she was still shaken by me shooting a gun near a guy I had trapped in the pool. We spoke little while eating. As Karen would be driving home, we drank water.

Before she left, I kissed her on the cheek. Our hands slid together. I said, "How about if we go on a date Saturday?"

The idea of us having a date, after our rowdy romps in bed, seemed to amuse Karen. "Where to?"

WHAT ABOUT REQUIRED READING /EXAMS for med school?

146

"How about Genoa Island? I rented a skiff. I want to see what it's like for someone to get on the island by boat, like Rattlesnake described."

Karen let go of my hand. "Stubborn, stubborn mule."

"We can check on Rattlesnake."

"Are you trying to bribe me?"

"Everything looks different on the river. You're at the center looking out. It's not to miss."

Karen punched me on the shoulder. Walking away, she said, "Don't try too hard. You might scare me off."

Burt Monsen greeted us on the dock, motorboats to his left and right. His brownish mustache was stringy, catfish-like. A life lived mostly under sunlight had given his cheeks a bronzed patina. I made the introductions. Karen climbed onto the metal skiff with her smooth glide.

Burt whispered, "Not too shabby." *expos.y*

I whispered, "Don't go there."

Karen did look regal in her straw hat and thin indigo long-sleeved pullover, cut-off jeans, killer legs and yellow tennis shoes. Burt handed our two bags to us on board, untied the rope, tossed it in and gave the skiff a foot shove. The current, which seemed slow from afar, carried us downstream. I yanked the short engine rope. The engine purred and sent ash-colored smoke behind us. I swiveled the motor, upped the throttle and just-like-that we moved through a silty river broad enough to carry ocean liners. Karen pressed a hand down on her straw hat. She'd thought ahead and had worked a narrow white scarf through slits on both sides, and tied the scarf across her Adam's apple. *WOMEN DON'T HAVE*

The boat's engine whirred pleasantly. Sitting in front, Karen faced forward. We passed outdoor breakfast diners sitting at tables *EM*

That's why they're CALLED ADAM's!

147

covered with white tablecloths, their ends gently swaying in the morning breeze; the California State Railroad Museum; a couple of large hotels that displayed American and California Bear flags. We crossed where the American River dumps its snowmelt load into the larger Sacramento. The levee road of Garden Highway appeared and paralleled the river. Houses on concrete stilts, raised above the flood line, seemed to float in mid-air. Plying upriver meant a steady fresh wind blew counter to our progress. Every few seconds, Karen's ponytail rose, then settled on the center of her sword-like spine.

Karen turned around on the front bench seat. She called above the whine of the engine. "I still say we should confront my uncle about hiring that guy to scare you off."

"He'll deny it."

"How can he," Karen said, "if I give him the name and address of Dennis McKay? If you'd kept his license, we'd really have him trapped."

I didn't say anything. A rush of wind gusted downstream. I thought of Clyde Whitney floating in the sky as a fount of pure contentment.

Karen said, "Besides always wanting to avoid conflict, you're kind of a loner, aren't you. I think that's why you never want any help. It's Jeff Taylor versus the world. Was it like that in basketball?"

"I was known as a team player. You can look it up."

Holding onto her Quaker-like straw hat, Karen spun around again, took in the view. Oak trees crowded the east bank. We passed the confluence of the Feather and Sacramento rivers. We traveled near the high bank of Genoa Island. Milky clouds, as big as mountains, hovered upriver.

The canal appeared on our right. It led to the Feather River at its other end, and was the long back line of the island's triangle. We motored from broad moving water into a kind of ditch about twenty feet across. I slackened the engine to a sputter. The canal's lanky walls were tangles of vegetation; its water, amber. Minnows fled both sides of the metal skiff.

Karen said, "Where are we going to stop?"

"Any place we can tie off and climb up. You could be on the lookout for something we might have trouble with."

"Like what?"

"A submerged stump. Chunks of concrete. Stuff like that."

"Now you tell me." Karen crawled onto the bow and held her body slightly overboard, looking into the water.

We moseyed along the canal. Its jungle-like walls were completely different than the dry flat plane of baking land above. We hadn't come close to the bridge attaching the island to the mainland when, to our right, an indentation in the canal wall appeared. From there a climb to the island was precipitous, but doable. I cut the engine, and used one of the oars tucked on board to guide us. With no current, it was easy to bring the skiff's nose onto soil and bushes springing from the canal's south bank. I tied us off. We filled Karen's day pack with items for Rattlesnake. She slipped it on. She stepped onto the steep hillside. I followed. There was no sign in the soil, nor torn branches, indicating anyone else had tied off there.

The steep climb left us huffing as we reached flat ground.

Bent over, Karen said, "How far to the mine?"

"The whole island is about two thousand acres. We'll find roads. Look, I brought a compass."

Still breathing hard, Karen said, "Oh wow. Taylor brought a compass."

I checked the compass and estimated the direction to Hotel Tin, which wasn't a gold mine as much as a soil collection station.

Every couple of hundred yards or so, we made markers of

branch mounds to follow back to the skiff. Rising sun raked across thirsty land. Digger pines and oak trees stood like sentries in the direction we walked. Their shadows fell sideways.

I said, "Are you having fun yet?"

"The votes aren't all in."

The day was proving to be what we needed, a lark, a passage of time without conflict, fear, or passion. Birds chattered. Lizards skittered over fallen leaves. We scooted around coyote bushes but tried to keep a straight line aiming at my guess for the ragged outpost.

I said, "We won't have trouble finding him."

"The more you say that, the less confident I become."

We approached the tree shadows. If our other time ambling on Genoa Island proved predictive, we'd find a trail that led to a dirt road. From there, follow the compass, consult the map I'd printed from the internet, and have a happy unexpected visit with Rattlesnake Johnson. His food basics covered, we'd stocked up on luxuries: jars of Greek olives, dried mangoes and apricots and, Karen's touch, California caviar from San Francisco Bay sturgeon to spread on gourmet crackers. Bringing the old guy surprise treats was a treat to ourselves. I imagined Rattlesnake's smile, his joy at gorging on food different from his usual bland fare.

A shot came from somewhere in the shadows. Birds shrieked and took flight.

I pulled Karen to the ground. "Stay flat."

Silence. On my belly, I tried to see into the shadows. Another shot rang out. Its sound hung in the air. I looked for cover. There was a clump of coyote bushes; they provided no protection. There, we'd be trapped. Looking back the way we came, I saw the last marker we'd made.

A third shot. Its sound indicated it came from closer to us than the other two.

I said, "He's coming our way." I had no clear idea how far away the shooter was. "We can't just wait for him. We run for it. Stay apart. Get ready."

Karen crawled up on her knees. She swiped away strands of hair and looked back to where we'd come from. I lifted the Giants baseball cap off my head.

"Now! Don't stop!"

I flung the cap sideways to momentarily distract the shooter. We sprinted toward the last marker. Pressure built between my shoulder blades—fear. A fourth shot rang out. Karen and I stumbled in unison, regained footing and ran as fast as we could. We raced past two markers of stacked brush. No more gunshots.

We settled into a jog. A calmness swept over me. Feeling in harmony with our surroundings, I said, "Clyde's here. I can feel it. It's reassuring."

Karen said, "Wake up. We just got shot at."

We reached the steep decline to the canal. I motioned to Karen to go first. We started down, grabbing Coyote bushes, bouncing our way toward the water. We reached the skiff. Karen climbed in, plopped onto the front bench seat. I unfastened the rope, stepped in and pushed off in a way that turned the metal boat in the direction we'd come. I looked up, saw nothing but hillside and sky. I yanked the engine's rope. The engine fired. I gave the throttle a twist; we headed off. A Great Blue Heron eyed us. It fluttered its huge wings and sailed just overhead.

Karen downed water in belching gulps. "Is it possible that was Rattlesnake? Wandering around the island, he hears something and just shoots?"

"That was a pistol, not a rifle. Besides, we were almost half a mile from his place."

"I wish you didn't know so much about guns."

"I don't. Just that the sounds didn't come from a Winchester rifle."

"Any idea who?"

"Somebody who thinks your grandfather has a treasure chest of gold on the island. That's who." Shaded most of the time, the air in the canal was cool. "Hal Bell thinks that, but he was never around guns that I know of. Dennis McKay knows the combinations to the locks through the rice paddies. The Little Feller got on the island before. It could be any of them. It's equally likely it's somebody else."

"Are you saying you don't know a damn thing?"

"That is correct." Inching up the throttle of the skiff, I said, "Please keep an eye out ahead."

At Burt's Boats, handing the rope to Burt, he looked us over. He'd rented hundreds of boats to thousands of people. He had surely developed a keen sense of how a trip on the river went.

Karen climbed out. I passed her the day pack.

Burt said, "How was the trip? Your clothes are kind of dusty, but sticky looking. You fall in?"

I laughed. I couldn't help it. "I fell in deep the day I met Karen. I've been falling one way or another ever since."

Karen looked to Burt. "We were dancing in the boat and fell in. We had to tow it to shore. It was sandy. Look, I even lost a shoe."

Burt and I looked. I hadn't noticed. She must have lost her right tennis shoe when we churned down the precipitous canal hillside, returning to the skiff.

Karen said to Burt, "Jeff makes me crazy."

I said, "Thank you."

Burt twisted an end of his catfish mustache. He said, "I don't believe a word of this."

I looked to Burt, and slowly shook my head. "Neither do I."

*

We went to my place, showered—Karen had some clothes and a pair of running shoes there—hopped into my car and headed out. I drove Garden Highway above the speed limit.

In the short term, calling the police would be a waste of time. The best we'd get was somebody filling out a form, and telling us to come in if we wanted to make a report. What did we have to tell? Four shots fired in a remote part of the county. No view of the shooter. Again and again, since throwing myself into pursuit of Clyde Whitney's rumored gold, it was like living in a dream where you can't get a handle on what's really happening.

Karen looked over at the speedometer. "Can't you drive faster?"

"Why didn't anybody ever get him a phone?"

"Grandpa got him one years ago. Rattlesnake wouldn't learn how to use it. Bell tried to talk him into a phone set up so all he has to do is press number one for him, two for Grandpa, and three for EMTs. Bell asked me to work on Rattlesnake. I got nowhere."

"I'll look into walkie-talkies. You just press and talk. He won't need to see or remember anything." *THERE SHORT DISTANCE*

We made good time. We clattered across the bridge. We rushed on a dusty road to the ramshackle arrangement of buildings called Heaven Mine. Henry Ford was not in sight. Neither was the yellow tabby. The Winchester rifle rested in its place against the cabin wall. I scoured the surrounding area, searching for anything suspicious. The car windows were down.

Karen opened the passenger door.

"Not yet." I pulled a switchblade from my jeans. I'd have been better equipped with the Smith & Wesson. As usual, Clint Sherman had known what he was talking about. "Let's sit here for a bit. Let's not walk into anything."

The cabin door opened. Rattlesnake popped into sunlight. The cat swooshed past his ankles. Rattlesnake flapped his right arm.

We called hellos from inside the car.

Rattlesnake's fingers scratched their way through the messy beard. "If you're looking for the kangaroo farm, it's down the road a piece." Rattlesnake giggled at his goofy words. "Hello, Karen. Hello, Jeff."

I kept watch on the cabin door. Rattlesnake crossed the porch, right knee swaying out, returning to center, and skipped down the two stairs. I searched his face for a hint something was amiss.

Rattlesnake said, "Since when did you two get so quiet?"

I climbed out of the car, eyes moving from the doorway to taking in as much as I could. I held the red-handled switchblade chest high. Karen opened a back door and reached in for her daypack.

She said, "We brought treats. Like for having a picnic. We thought it would be fun to surprise you."

Karen carried the daypack. I stayed on the lookout for intruders. We walked toward the wood buildings.

Rattlesnake said, "You picked a good one. It's not so hot today."

Karen unpacked what we'd packed in the boat. We sat at the old wood picnic table. We ate. My thoughts were elsewhere.

Rattlesnake's milky eyes swam with delight at dipping crackers into California caviar. "It's been a long time since I ate something like this." He dipped, ate. Bits of caviar stuck to his gray beard. "I can't thank you both enough. I try not to complain. I like the privacy, but from time to time I do get lonesome out here."

I said, "Rattlesnake, how well do you know the island? The whole two thousand acres."

"I used to have a lot of it memorized. It's faded, because I don't walk it like before I lost my eyes. Use it or lose it, they say. I bet the same goes for your hand."

"Precisely," I said.

Rattlesnake's eyes tightened. "Precisely why you asking me this stuff?"

"You said the Little Feller must have come by boat. I'm wondering how well you remember the canal going toward the Sacramento River."

Rattlesnake's face scrunched together. "From the bridge to the Sacramento, I'd say I remember half. No, less than that. You got to remember, the canal runs two miles end to end. It's mostly disappeared from my memory."

Karen said, "It seems like the guy who surprised you, and searched the cabin—it seems like he might have come that way. It'd be easier than going up current against the Feather and then over. Ever hear motorboats from that direction?"

"Sure. A couple times a year. People even turn up at the mine. They've never been a problem, till the Little Feller. They look around, and I assume think I'm just an old coot living all alone." Rattlesnake added, "Nobody thinks about gold being down here. It's all up in the hills, right? That's what people think."

Karen said, "We're worried about someone coming around and causing you trouble, now that Grandpa's passed on."

Rattlesnake said, "Who knows how many vultures think they might cash in. He's kind of a legend. A big shot space satellite man walks away from it, comes West to get dirty like the rest of us."

We ate off paper plates we'd brought, along with fresh paper napkins. Stomachs full, we relaxed in our chairs, listening to birds and the slight breeze.

Trying to sound nonchalant, I said, "Did you hear any gunshots today? On our way in, I thought I heard a gun go off."

Rattlesnake said, "I heard some a few hours ago, not now. That'd be fellers shooting rabbits in the paddies. They're drained five months a year. They attract rabbits like flies to honey." Rattlesnake flashed a triumphant grin. "Takes more skill to catch 'em like I do. Will you excuse me for a minute?"

Rattlesnake disappeared inside the cabin. I got up and walked around the porch, still on the lookout for something suspect.

Karen said, "What do you think about the rabbit hunting?"

"I'm sure it's true. But that's not what happened with us."

The more time I spent at the run-down mess of a place called Heaven Mine, the more I felt its uniqueness. The idea of Stan Whitney turning it into a resort disgusted me.

Rattlesnake emerged from the cabin. He brandished two keys. "If we're going to start living on caviar and fancy olives, you two need to find a pile."

We found one baggy. Considering it was our third search of the area, that wasn't surprising. My thinking was that since Clyde hid his methods from Bell, and everyone, he would have done the same with the results.

Twenty

Dr. Fisher was the reason I contacted Greg Naugle. I couldn't evade his words: "You're failing yourself." What kind of doctor ignored the emotional pain of a man fighting cancer, and who confessed his personal failure? What kind of doctor would I become if I clung to my victimhood?

I sent Greg Naugle an email. Email allowed us to give more thought to our words than during a phone call. His reply took a day to arrive. He offered to drive to Sacramento. He suggested we meet at the park where we'd first met, and walk to any nearby café for lunch. Never on the basketball court, no matter the situation, had I been as fidgety and nervous as that noon.

Naugle walked with both hands in his pockets. Neither of us looked the other in the eye. He extended his right hand. I shook it. He caught himself glancing at my hook of a hand, then he looked straight at me. I fought the urge to flee.

He said, "Thanks for meeting me." He wore a short-sleeved beige shirt, the cords of the other time in the park. His light eyes were livelier. "I know this isn't easy for you."

"I need more proof than researching where you grew up."

Naugle said, "In the middle of your mother's back is a blue birthmark. It's an oval. I'll talk about anything you want."

A large part of me didn't want to talk about anything. And I didn't need proof; I knew he was my dad. I was stalling.

He said, "You were a hell of a basketball player. I missed it all." Naugle looked to the grass. "That was dumb. I wouldn't have cared if you were ranked last on the chess team. I screwed up."

"Let's go have lunch."

He said, "I'm buying."

I said, "It's about time."

"You got me there."

We went, without conversation, to River City Café, where I sometimes took my laptop and studied. Small, intimate, it featured an array of sandwiches. Naugle seemed impressed when Stefano, the owner, called me by name and walked us to a table. That's when things got uncomfortable. We both asked for water. I looked at the familiar menu though didn't read it. I wondered if I was just going through the motions to make myself feel like I was doing the right thing. I felt no desire to get to know Greg Naugle.

Naugle took a sip of ice water, then rattled the ice cubes in his glass. "My son's going to be a junior. He plays basketball and baseball. He'd kill to be half the star you were."

I said, "What do you want to know?"

"I came here wondering what you wanted to know."

"I'm not sure. What I do know is, you never tried to contact me until you got sick."

All color drained from Naugle's face. He drank more water. He looked at the tabletop. "I don't claim otherwise."

An image of Clyde Whitney, smiling beneath the enveloping branches of a majestic willow tree, came to mind. It sent a message: be kind. I said, "I don't want to hurt your feelings. At the same time, I don't want to pretend I'm interested in getting to know you."

Stefano came to the table. Thickset, dark haired, he took his food and his customers with utmost seriousness.

I looked at this man who was my biological father. "How about tuna sandwiches? I don't know what he does with them, but they're great."

"Sounds good."

Stefano made swift notations on the receipt pad as he left.

Naugle cleared his throat. "How's your mother doing?"

"I guess she's fine. We don't keep in touch very often. She moved to Alaska right after I graduated from high school."

"That must have been rough."

I shrugged. "She left everything behind, pregnant at nineteen and didn't believe in abortion. When she was thirty-seven, and had a shot at adventure, she went for it. It hurt like hell at the time. Now I see she deserved to have her own life."

The sandwiches, made before opening at eleven, came. This gave us something to occupy ourselves with. In the silence of sharing food, a thin slice of the hardened chip on my shoulder fell away.

"Where's the disease?"

He poured ice water from a glass pitcher. "Left lung. In my twenties, I took in tons of smoke. Today's buildings are toxin boxes. If you don't wear good PPE, it can catch up to you. We didn't take it seriously enough back then. Macho nonsense."

"Treatment?"

"I began radiation three weeks ago. I'm on medical leave. That's how I've been able to come up here so much."

"Is it painful?"

"I get short of breath. Not being able to breathe makes you think about the end. It gets you thinking about everything."

I said, "A month ago, I met somebody who had a major effect on me. I probably didn't spend more than four hours total with him. But every time I saw him was meaningful. He was my girlfriend's grandfather. He got me thinking about things. He died. I miss him, even though I barely knew him." I found myself talking as much to myself as across the table. "I don't know why I'm telling you this."

Naugle said, "Would you be comfortable telling me more?"

It turned out I was. I told Naugle about Clyde, from the moment he wandered into Dr. Fisher's office until he was recovered from the pond at Willow Park. The more I talked about Clyde, the lighter I felt. The nervousness abated. Naugle was interested enough to ask questions, especially when I described Clyde's belief that everything has happened before, not just once, but in an endless cycle from the big bang to what we think of as the end of time. Then the big bang and billions of years repeat, exactly as before.

I said, "Now I get what Hindus mean when they describe life as a cosmic joke."

Naugle said, "Well, one thing about having cancer, you don't think of life as a joke. I sure don't."

The pitcher of ice water empty, Naugle paid, left a big tip and we walked into the heat of an August Sacramento afternoon. At the corner, we shook hands and walked in opposite directions. Our goodbyes were smothered by the rumblings of a city bus pushing its weight ahead at the changing of a stoplight. No mention of meeting again.

Growing up, I had imaginary conversations with an amorphous, imagined father. I'd yell at him, tell him how much he'd hurt me. A couple of conversations I memorized, to be at the ready if the time ever came. The time had come. My father turned out to be a decent guy suffering from lung cancer at forty-eight years old.

Twenty-one

Karen and I planned to have dinner at her place. I got there before she did. Stan and Laura were back from New York. My phone showed Stan's SUV at his office. Laura's sleek green Jaguar wasn't around. I went to the main house's rear, pressed the bell and endured the booming concert.

Katia answered. Her blue eyes burned like sparklers, not in celebration.

I said, "I'm trying to decide if I should tell Stan and Laura about you being in Clyde's guesthouse. And catching you with some of his gold."

"I was just cleaning. Don't make things up."

"Okay. But do you think Hal Bell was making it up when he told me he drove you here that night? Parked his truck out on the street?"

Bell never said that. I was attempting to stir up dishonor among thieves. The irony that Karen and I were sitting on approaching a hundred thousand dollars in poached gold dust was not lost on me.

Katia's teeth chomped together. They let go. "Tell Whitneys whatever you want. They know I'm a good worker."

"I was talking about Hal Bell. He says he dropped you off here that night."

"Mr. Bell wouldn't say that."

"No? He even asked me to keep an eye on you. Bell thinks you'll keep anything for yourself, even though he was the one who let you know Clyde might have gold tucked away."

"Bell can go to hell. You can go to hell."

"I'll give you two days, forty-eight hours, to decide if you'll talk to me or I go to Stan with catching you stealing in Clyde's place. Is that clear?"

"I go back to cleaning this giant house."

Katia slammed the door on me. Perfect. Let her stew. If she got scared, she might want to talk. After all, I hadn't told Stan and Laura about her digging around Clyde's guesthouse when she thought no one was around. The idea was to get her to trust me more than she trusted Hal Bell.

I lounged poolside, thinking through people and situations. Foremost was worrying about Rattlesnake Johnson. Could we leave him out there, after the gunshots?

Karen walked up the mauve tinted concrete path. She carried her daypack in hand. A smile illuminated her face. I left the chair, kissed Karen and held her close.

I said, "Why so happy all of a sudden?"

"I'm happy life is settling down. I'm able to focus on school. I'm happy to be back in California, where we're together."

"Speaking of *not* being together, where's Aunty Rae? Wasn't she going to bring her team to the state fair for horse races? What happened?"

"Who knows. The pattern is, every time she has a blowout with family, she disappears."

"You think she'll be racing?"

"If she enters any races, she won't tell any of us unless she wins. Then she'll be here in a flash."

Karen set the daypack on the round glass table. She took a seat. I said, "I looked into walkie-talkies. The best ones have a range up to thirty miles. In a straight line, Rattlesnake is about twenty-two miles from here. Twenty-seven from my house."

The orange specks in Karen's eyes joined the radiance of her face. "All he can do is say no."

The store with the most choices in walkie-talkies was *Sacramento Firearms, Gear and Hand-Helds,* housed in a long, one-story building located south of downtown. I went there first thing the next morning. The store's website claimed it stocked more hand-held radio devices than any other store in America. It also sold an array of handguns, rifles and ammo. I took a few loops in the parking lot before landing a space. At the store's entrance, a 300-pound guard, with a reddish beard shaped like a spear, asked if I was carrying. He patted me down before allowing me to go inside.

I found a sign reading "WTs HERE!" A young woman, hair dyed a dazzling chartreuse, presided over the glass counter. She asked what I wanted. I didn't know what I wanted. The young woman educated me as to options. I bought three walkie-talkies and was relieved when the clerk didn't say my credit card wouldn't go through.

The walkie-talkies were easy to set up as a network. The woman at the counter, which was not bustling like the firearms sections, did it for me. You simply pressed and talked. All three were active at once; there was no choosing one over another. Their range was, in theory, thirty miles. Because the land involved was flat, I was assured they'd perform just fine.

On the way home I thought of another way to search for spots Clyde Whitney may have stashed gold dust. During the years I was with Sherman Investigations, I'd gotten to know Marcia Hall, who worked in the county assessor's office. Sixtyish, curt, she was all business the first few times I needed to do research. That changed. It turned out that for a fifty-dollar bill Marcia would let me dig around any records and ledgers I desired, for as long as I desired. I think the money made her feel naughty. I drove up the numbered streets, pulled onto Highway 50. Three exits later, I got off and parked in front a trio of squat chunky concrete buildings that housed the county assessor's office, the tax collector's office, and voter registration.

I entered the assessor's office at shortly after nine o'clock.

Marcia popped up from a desk set back from a high dark Formica counter that separated the public from the public records. We shook hands. Her smile was tremendous. Marcia gave my hand a glance.

"Still there," I said.

We chatted. I told her I was in medical school. Marcia said she was midway through her last year before retirement.

She said, "It's so good to see you."

"That goes both ways."

Marcia snatched a Kleenex, removed her glasses and wiped her eyes. "Jeff, you did it. You're going to be a doctor."

Marcia had let her hair go gray, with bangs reaching granny glasses. Thinning straight hair dangled down her back. She presided over the city's parcel maps, road maps, topographic maps, most anything still on paper.

Marcia blew her nose. Sniffed. "Okay. I'm done. What do you need?"

"I need a map, or maps, of Genoa Island. Do you know it?"

Marcia took a step back. Somehow, I'd knocked her off stride. "What do you think I've been doing here all these years? Have a seat at one of the tables. I'll bring it to you."

Marcia brought me an oversized book of survey maps. Carrying it required outstretched arms. Genoa Island filled three pages. By then I was familiar enough with it to easily follow the sketchy maps. Improvements, from times past, were written in by hand. I figured that was related to tax assessments. Little boxes denoted the original cabins. An original bridge was shown next to Clyde's replacement. I knew this because the bridges on the plat map had 1947 and 2002 written above them. Hotel Tin was not indicated. This told me Clyde had built it without a permit. That made sense because to get permission to take water from the river, flow it through his silt-filled sluice box, then send much of the water back, would have required an environmental impact report and expensive compliances to state regulations. It struck me as just like Clyde Whitney to go his own way.

Turning pages, following the island southeast, I came upon a circle, half an inch in diameter. Inscribed within it: BS. Below the circle was printed 1963.

I went to Marcia's counter and asked her to look at something with me. We passed a couple who perused a ledger, and went to the table where the map of a portion of Genoa Island lay open. Marcia twirled a section of her bangs around her forefinger.

I said, "What's with this BS?"

Marcia said, "Excuse me?"

"The old buildings are marked. Some roads are inked in. The original bridge and its replacement. But what's the BS mean?"

Marsha threw me a terse look. I put my finger on the little circle.

Marcia said, "For a second there, I thought you'd changed on me." She lifted her glasses a tad above her nose, leaned in close for a good look. "I haven't seen one of these in years. I only know what it is from my original training. BS stands for bomb shelter. As in an underground bomb shelter.

"Bomb shelter?"

"Note the nineteen sixty-three. The year after the Cuban Missile Crisis. Do you know what that is?"

"Even an ex jock like me knows that. But how does it end up on a county map?"

"That's a good question. I was told people who had a bomb shelter installed on their land often came in to make sure it got recorded. That way, somebody might know where to look for them after a nuclear war."

I said, "I can tell you're not joking."

"That was serious stuff back then. People who owned that much land had money, and got bomb shelters installed. Those old buildings would be weekend getaway cabins for wealthy city people. Why are you so interested?"

"I shouldn't get into that."

Marcia said, "It's really good to see you again."

She returned to her work space. I took out my phone and clicked pictures of the three maps. I carried the plat book to the front counter. I had only a twenty and a five in my wallet. I looked around. The other three people in the room of tables and chairs peered down at maps. I reached over the chest-high Formica counter and let the money drop onto a lower counter behind it.

Marcia seemed to be feigning involvement with paperwork.

I said, "Live long and be happy."

I headed toward the hallway.

Marcia called after me, "Jeff? Could I talk to you for a second?"

"Of course."

Marcia and I arrived at the front counter simultaneously. She surveyed the people busy looking over plat maps.

Marcia whispered, "I'm not supposed to do this, but it's too late to fire me."

"Not supposed to…?"

"Talk about people who come in and look at county materials."

I whispered, "I understand."

Marcia twirled a lock of gray bangs dangling in front of the left lens of her glasses. "Just before we closed yesterday, two men asked to see the plat book with Genoa Island maps. Besides you, and them, the last time my records show anyone looking at the book was twenty years ago."

"That long?"

"That long ago. I'll never forget the man. He emitted a glow. I don't mean shiny skin, but something glowing from inside. It freaked me out."

I refrained from mentioning Clyde. I said, "You never ask me for it, but did one of these guys yesterday need to give you ID before checking out the plat book?"

"It's against the law to demand identification, or a reason someone wants to view public materials."

"Remember what they looked like?"

"They stood out, because they kept looking over their shoulders, like they were afraid someone might catch them being here."

"One was maybe thirties, big muscles?"

"Yep."

"Was the other one smaller?"

Marcia emitted a rare titter. "Not just smaller. About the same age. A very polite little man. He did the talking for both of them. He's no more than five-two. My height. I haven't weighed as little as he does since about eighth grade."

I looked around, and spoke softly. "Anything else?"

"The other guy? With all the muscles? He looked right through me, like I was made of air. Whatever you're up to, be careful."

Twenty-two

How did McKay and the Little Feller end up forming an alliance? For the moment it didn't matter. What mattered was beating them to the bomb shelter, a logical place for Clyde to store his gold. I didn't think they would hurt Rattlesnake; the bomb shelter was far enough away from his cabin he wouldn't even hear a vehicle driving to it. Still, it was a near certainty one of those guys had a gun. There were two of them, one of me. I needed help.

Sitting in the parking lot outside the assessor's office, I took up my phone with the intention of calling Sherman Investigations. Clint could call around for backup. I clicked off before the first ring. I didn't have time to wait for Clint to find assistance. I called someone else.

"Hello, Jeff. What a nice surprise."

"I need your help."

Greg Naugle's tone changed from casual to all business. "Anything. What do you need? Does it have to do with you being followed?"

I started the car and headed for home. I told Naugle a short-version answer to his question of why I was being followed. I gave him directions going north on Garden Highway to the road leading past the rice paddies. "I'll be ahead of you. I'll close the gate, but the locks won't be engaged. I'll leave a walkie-talkie in the grass by the left gate post, the opposite side of the locks. You click the on button and it stays on all the time. We can communicate without interruption."

"I'm heading to my car right now."

The code when you get to the bridge is one-eight-four-four-zero."

"Got it. One-eight-four-four-zero."

"You sure you're good with this?"

"I'm good with it."

I heard the engine of his car start.

I said, "There's only one road in from Garden Highway. It goes past drained rice paddies. When you cross the bridge to the island, go straight. Ignore any side roads. Go straight till you reach a group of old buildings. An older guy named Rattlesnake will come out and won't recognize you by sound. He's blind. Tell him Karen Brady and Jeff sent you. Tell him you're there to keep the Little Feller from nosing around. He'll understand. I'll get on the walkie talkie when needed."

"Rattlesnake? The Little Feller? You lost me."

"Tell you later."

Naugle said, "I'll be on Highway 5 in five minutes."

"Thanks."

Naugle said, "I got to watch the road now." He hung up.

I texted Karen: *Going to Genoa. Need lock combos ASAP. Will get back to you.*

They came before I reached the freeway.

I parked at the curb in front of the brick bungalow. I saw each brick in the front wall separately, reminding me of Clyde's telling Karen, when she was a child, to look at a lawn one grass blade at a time. Inside, I grabbed my red-handled switchblade, a flashlight, baseball bat and a plastic bottle of water. I dumped them on the Jetta's backseat and headed for the Sacramento River.

I'd never seen a police car on Garden Highway. I drove its levee miles as fast as I could keep control. I crossed the Feather River, pulled off and unlocked the two combination locks. I pushed open the painted-white steel gate, left a walkie-talkie in weeds, and shut but did not lock the gate behind me.

I raced past the three rice paddies that were like craters dipping below the desolate land. At the gate to the island, I entered the five-digit code. The gate slowly groaned, its small hard rubber wheels pulling open the tall fence topped with barbed wire. Progressing on the island, I took the first left, one of many island roads I'd never been on.

Ping. Karen.

I tapped the phone. I said, "I'm pretty sure I found where Clyde and Henry Ford took the gold. There's a nineteen sixties bomb shelter, not far from the Feather River. I saw it on maps at the assessor's office."

Karen's voice surged. "That's incredible. That's great!"

"Except McKay and the Little Feller beat me to it. They looked at the same map late yesterday."

"They're working together?"

"They are now." The road became dense with weeds. Like the rest of Genoa Island, built up with silt from the hydraulic mining days, there were few rocks. Weeds slapped the underside of the moving car.

Karen said, "Be careful."

I said goodbye. According to the maps, it was about a mile to the bomb shelter. Heavy-looking oak trees were joined by digger pines on both sides of the silty road. Then the road sliced through the first stretch of true forest I'd seen on Genoa Island, lime-green digger pines planted so close together you couldn't see through them. They must have been planted that way, to block sight lines, sixty years ago. I came upon the white Ram 2500 pickup. Nobody was in it, at least that I could see. It took a few back-and-forths to turn the car around in case I'd need a quick escape. I emptied my pockets of all keys, coins, and instructions for the walkie-talkies. I put my phone in a back pocket, the flashlight in one front pocket, the switchblade in the other. I grabbed the aluminum baseball bat.

I checked the big pickup's doors. Locked. I whipped out the switchblade and squatted next to the bulky front left tire. I employed a technique I'd learned from a guy at Sherman Investigations. I jammed the tip of the knife blade into the tire's sidewall and turned the blade in a circle, creating a hole rather than a slit. A rushing wind sound shot from the tire. On that desolate terrain it carried louder than I expected but there was no turning back. I punctured the left rear tire the same way. I worried McKay might hear the sounds.

From the photos I'd taken of the island maps, I knew to go to the right. I walked between trees and came to a narrow path. I stopped. Listened. Escaping air sounds from the tires could no longer be heard. I heard no voices, no footsteps. I saw a broken branch. I ducked under it and two minutes later reached a small clearing. What looked like the open lid of a coffin, albeit a thin steel one, was in the center of the clearing. On the ground were three locks, strung with thick wire, snapped and laid across the ground in a line paralleling the open hatch. Next to that lay bolt cutters.

Welded at each inside corner of the cover was a handle for pushing it open from inside.

I called Clint Sherman and gave him my location. I told him about the unlocked white gate and the empty rice paddies. I gave him the code to the bridge gate. I asked Clint to call the sheriff's department, because they'd respond to him right away and not to me, and tell them I was observing a major robbery in progress.

"It's the guy who stomped me. He probably has an accomplice."

Clint's froggy voice: "I'm on it." He hung up.

I'd hide in the trees and wait for backup.

My thoughts didn't race out of control, like they used to.

Why did I call Naugle? Why get him mixed up in something that could escalate into danger? To show him I was worthy, that he'd been wrong to keep me out of his life. That thought led to realizing I'd equally called Naugle to show him I believed *he* was worthy, and I needed him.

Only then did I remember the walkie-talkie in the car. Should I go back for it? I didn't want to lose sight of the bomb shelter's opening.

I focused on the present. If McKay, or McKay and the Little Feller came out before anyone showed, should I hide and follow them, or should I go after McKay's back with the baseball bat?

Hiding was no good. McKay would see my car.

A feminine voice carried up the shaft of the bomb shelter. "Don't! Dennis! Please don't!"

The voice cried out in pain. I walked closer to the opened hatch. The feminine voice begged McKay to leave her alone. I went to the shaft. An acidic scent drifted upwards. No more sounds ascended from underground. This alarmed me.

A moaning came from below, then someone crying out in pain again.

Sadistic bastard, I thought.

I pointed the aluminum baseball bat straight ahead. Channeled sunlight led me down steel stairs. After eight was a landing where a steel hatch had been opened and attached to a hook alongside the stairs. I attempted to keep my steps quiet, but they echoed in the slender canyon. I didn't care. McKay likely wasn't armed and this way he had no chance run off. I'd use the bat on the bastard without hesitation.

A second run of eight stairs and I faced a steel wall that reached the ceiling, which was probably eight feet high. Still, no sounds. To the right, an opening about six feet wide. I raised the bat. I stepped through the opening ready to swing it. A small flashlight lived on what I made out to be a small square steel table. I didn't see a soul.

Dennis McKay's voice came through darkness. "Set the bat down. Reach for the ceiling. Palms forward."

He fired a gun. I hit the deck. The sound reverberated in my ears. The baseball bat clattered against the steel floor and rolled away. I got to my feet, put my hands up.

Dennis McKay laughed. "That makes us even, asshole."

Light exploded to my left. A potent flashlight. It was in McKay's left hand. In his right hand was a pistol.

On the opposite side of the steel wall at the bottom of the stairs were steel cupboards with *Water*, *Supplies* and *Medicine* painted in black on their doors. They were partially open. McKay set the flashlight on the table. The table had one chair. To both sides, beds with bare mattresses were built into the walls. Sleeping bags, still in their plastic store covers of more than half a century ago, were one to a bed. There was a sink but no faucet.

McKay's cat's eyes shined. "Hey Calder," he said, "did you see how fast this asshole kissed the floor?"

A sweet voice, clear, articulate: "I don't wish to engage in conversation with you." Light and feathery, the voice was a male's.

Following the voice, I located a small figure roped onto a metal chair against the far wall. His hands were tied to the back of the chair.

Again, McKay laughed. "Keep your hands up, buddy. Don't get sloppy on me."

The pungent smell of Nitroglycerin, from the gunshot, joined the acidic smells of the underground steel container. Keeping the gun on me, McKay swept an arm under the table. Out came a duffel bag. McKay gripped its handle with his left hand. He hoisted it as if gauging its weight.

A calmness settled inside me.

McKay said, "Not so chatty when the tables are turned, huh?"

I didn't respond.

The man in the corner, surely Calder, said, "Dennis, I'm having a difficult time remaining in this creepy locale."

McKay waved the gun toward one of the side-wall beds. He said, "Asshole, go stand over there. Face the wall. Keep your hands high."

I did this.

The smaller man said, "Sincerely, this is not humorous."

McKay said, "I'll tell you what's funny. I'm going to leave you two here. You'll have food and water for a about a month. You'll get familiar with the pit toilet."

The Little Feller said, "Please don't be like this."

Facing the wall, I heard McKay move through the steel tomb. Footsteps pounded steel stairs. They stopped. A few seconds later, a heavy-sounding *thunk* reverberated throughout the bomb shelter. As it diminished, a distinct metal-on-metal sound; McKay sealed the stairwell hatch.

I took out my phone. No reception. I walked the room, clicked the phone off, tried again. And again.

"Mr. Taylor, was that noise what I think it is?"

"I'll go see."

"After you take a look, could you be so kind as to untie me?"

I slipped out my flashlight and followed its narrow light through the opening that led to the bottom of the stairs. I shined the light up them.

I called to the other end of the bomb shelter. "The hatch is down. That's what the sound was."

"Are we trapped?"

"I don't know." A round steel band, an inch below the hatch, showed in the light. I said, "Just curious. Are you a jockey?"

"Retired."

Returning to the main room, I shined the light on Calder, seated at the back wall. "You're working for Aunty Rae, aren't you."

"I am not. We share our love. We train the horses together. RaeLynn won't let me race anymore. She's concerned I might become scathed."

I grabbed the top of the steel chair, pulled it away from the wall and turned it sideways. Marcia was right: Calder didn't weigh much. "How did you and McKay team up?"

I took out my switchblade.

Calder's eyes flashed. Swelling and redness, and a little blood, showed at both temples. He said, "Dennis and I kept seeing each other in the hospital parking lot. He finally came over and said we should talk. Dennis can be quite persuasive."

"What made you think to go to the county?"

Calder grinned like a child licking a Popsicle. "You'll like this. Two nights ago, I'm watching an old movie at the hotel. *Chinatown*. You know it?"

I said no.

Calder said, "It's really, really good. In it, Jack Nicholson goes to the county to get information on who owns certain pieces of land. So I'm thinking, why not go to the county, see what we can find out about the island? Dennis and I spent most of yesterday going from office to office. They're not in the same building half the time. Then we hit the jackpot."

I put the small flashlight away. "I'm going to cut the rope.

Don't get any ideas."

"Oh, I've changed sides. Dennis turned out to be an unreliable sort. In fact, I have information I believe you will find noteworthy."

I set the other flashlight to shine light on the rope. I sawed between his wrists. The white rope frayed. The sawing sounded like I was cutting into soft wood.

Calder said, "That pistol Dennis has? It contains only blanks. I'd never shoot a real bullet at anything. Like with you and your lady friend. It was all blanks."

Sawing, I said, "Why didn't you say something? I had a baseball bat."

"And get hit on the head again? No, thank you. I gathered up all the gold, forty-three packets. They were in corners, under the beds, all over the place. I dug around in the cupboards. Does Dennis thank me? No. He takes my pistol and hits me with it on the side of the head. He ties me to the chair. Rather tautly, I might add."

I found a rhythm, pulling harder on downward slices. The rope cut quickly. "How did you know Karen and I were on the island when you shot the damn blanks?"

Calder said, "I'd landed close to the bridge. I heard an engine in the canal. It got so I was going out there most every day, looking for what turned out to be here. This was before I teamed up with Dennis. I followed the sound. Now that we've cleared that up, how do you propose we get out of here?"

"I have no idea."

I freed his hands. Calder stood, rotated his wrists. A short, compact man, he exuded strength and energy. I'd read where jockeys are often great natural athletes, just too small to compete in the major sports.

I handed Calder my small flashlight and headed for the stairs. We left the baseball bat. We left the larger flashlight burning. I climbed steel stairs to the landing with the hatch down. It was about five feet high in there. I stooped to get under it. Calder shined the light from behind me.

I reached back. Like passing a baton, Calder slapped the pocket flashlight into the palm of my left hand. I transferred it to my right hand. "I don't think they'd build something where you can accidentally lock yourself in. There. I see. I just need to unscrew this metal hoop. Undo what he did on top."

Calder said, "One time, when I was little, I crawled under the house and got stuck. I've been a mite claustrophobic ever since."

"Not now. Keep the light on my hands."

I passed the light backwards. Calder shined it on my hands. The steel circle, somewhat larger than a basketball hoop, wouldn't budge. It probably hadn't been turned from underneath in decades, as Clyde would have gone in without dropping the hatch behind him. The only reason to drop it would be to avoid radiation.

I fought the hoop. I pounded it with my good hand, hoping to break the seal.

I said, "Let's switch. You've got two good hands."

I stepped backwards, left side of the stairs. Calder handed me the light and stepped onto the landing. He smelled of a spicy perfume.

Calder said, "Which direction?"

"I'm thinking right, because on top he probably sealed it to the right, like you screw in lightbulbs and stuff."

Calder grabbed the hoop and fought it like I did. He grunted. He backed up a foot to get under it at a better angle. He heaved. And heaved.

I said, "Harder! Get us out of here!"

A raspy, scraping sound from above. Calder contorted his body, groaned and got the hoop turning. He let out a roar and turned the hoop until it wouldn't go any farther.

I said, "Get all the way under it. Raise it. There's a hook to secure it. You hold it up. I'll reach up and hook it."

I joined Calder on the landing. Our bodies pressed against one another. My shirt became soaked with sweat. I put the flashlight into my left jeans pocket, facing up. The light was feeble but enough.

"Okay. Lift. You got to get it high."

The little man had power; the hatch rose. I got my right forearm under it and helped. The hatch folded upward toward the wall. The hook was big and designed to fit over the steel hoop on top of the hatch. A ringing metal-hitting-metal sound; the hatch was secured. It hung six inches out from the side wall.

Light shot into the stairwell. McKay hadn't bothered to shut the coffin lid, though we could have opened it using the steel handles. I assumed he figured we were doomed.

I climbed out, opened and closed my eyes, adjusting to earthly light. Behind me, Calder let out a moaning sigh.

I said, "Pick it up. I gave him two flat tires. He won't be too far ahead to catch."

Twenty-three

We whizzed through patches of tall grass. I lowered the windows. Warm wind brushed my face. I saw everything with utter clarity.

This included, in glances, Calder. Long dark hair bounced in time with the bouncing of the car. His eyes were dark. His teal button-down shirt looked expensive. His hands were thick with callouses. His fingernails, however, were tended to as completely as any diva's. He looked like a super fit sixth grader with the face of a man in his latter thirties.

Calder said, "Now that I've switched sides, I wish to share something with you."

I'd known the guy about ten minutes and was already weary of him.

Calder said, "What Dennis did to that nice old gentleman should not go unpunished. There was no cause. Except I guess greed."

Eyes on the road, I drove as fast as I dared. "Continue."

"Dennis and I went to the Whitney place. If no one was there, we were going to look for gold. He'd quit working for Whitney, but he had keys. There were cars, so we left. Dennis points to an old gentleman walking on the other side of the street. He pulls over, calls Whitney by his first name. Whitney says the darnedest thing. He says, 'Have you come to take me to my maker?'"

179

We left the overgrown stretch of the road and spun over pure silt.

"Dennis tells him that's why we're there. The old guy is overjoyed. Dennis gets out, escorts the man to the passenger door. I scoot over. Whitney gets in and we head off. Dennis asks where he'd like to go to heaven from. Whitney says he was going to a place called Willow Pond, hoping for just that. He says, 'Turn right, I think.'"

I looked ahead for the right turn I'd have to take. If I missed it there was no chance of catching McKay.

"Dennis says, 'I need to know this is really you. Where did you store the gold?' Whitney's all joy. He says something about heaven's ceiling being filled with gold. Dennis reminds Whitney he's *going* to heaven, but his gold isn't there yet. Whitney concentrates really hard. I can tell he's trying to please Dennis. He says, 'I don't remember, except you go down to it. Under the ground. Can you find it, and take it to my maker?'"

"What did McKay say to that?"

"He said that was God's will. Whitney's so happy he looks twenty years younger. We get to the place with the willow trees. No one's around. The old guy gets out. He's weeping with joy.

"Dennis walks him across the grass. Whitney says, 'Bless you.' Dennis walks him right into the water. Dennis holds him down. It was weird. The man didn't struggle. He didn't make one splash."

I stomped the accelerator. The peaceful clarity I'd been living in vaporized. I turned right. We reached the bridge gate. I punched in the code.

I said, "Why didn't you stop him?"

Calder said, "I'm sorry. I was scared of—"

He didn't get to finish his sentence. I smacked Calder across the mouth with my hook hand, watched the gate open, and raced off. "Why end his life? For God's sake, *why*?"

Calder shimmied side-to-side. He sighed dramatically. "Dennis didn't want to take the chance of Whitney telling anybody else. He figured we'd find the place sooner or later."

Naugle's voice shot out of the walkie-talkie, placed in the food slot between the front seats. Well ahead, I caught sight of the white pickup.

Naugle said, "I'm in. I can see the first paddy. I left the gate unlocked in case we need to get out fast."

"McKay's headed your way. He's crazy. Avoid him."

The white pickup moved at a leisurely speed, tilted leftward on the two flats. I cranked the Jetta up to fifty. Then sixty on the gravelly terrain. I closed the gap between us and the pickup. McKay must have seen the Jetta in his rearview mirror because he sped up. The distance between us tightened. I passed the first empty rice paddy.

Naugle, on the walkie-talkie: "I see him."

"Don't try to stop him."

I saw McKay look into the rearview mirror.

Over the walkie-talkie: "He's coming at me."

"Swerve left into the grass."

Naugle drove straight at McKay. At the last possible instant, the red Subaru swept left into pale dead grass. In reaction, McKay swerved left. His accelerating speed, and the two flat tires, combined to make the swerve an overcorrection. The white whale of a pickup lurched onto the slope of the drained rice paddy. It bobbled across the rougher ground. Gradually, like a ship going over the horizon, it disappeared. In the rearview mirror I saw Naugle race a half circle in reverse. The Subaru caught the road and headed after me.

Calder said, "Sir, please slow down."

McKay turned the truck back up the grade of the second rice paddy. I saw its hood. Then the whole vehicle. It churned below and to the left. The engine seemed to explode with noise. Chunks of soil flew backwards as he headed up the grade.

I slowed, trying to decide what to do. If I cut McKay off, he'd plough right through the Jetta.

Calder said, "Thank you."

"Shut up."

The right front tire of the Ram 2500 slammed into the culvert that drained the rice paddy every year. The truck's right front rose, like an elephant rearing back and flipping up its enormous head. The truck teetered on the two flat left tires, crossing the slope of the rice paddy's wall. Slowly, inexorably, its weight on that incline toppled the white Ram 2500. The skidding crash sounded like a train wreck. The driver's door was pinned shut. The passenger door faced skyward. A plume of black smoke curled sideways from under the hood.

I stopped, and stepped out into swirling dust.

Calder got out. He said, "Oh my goodness."

Sunlight bounced off the truck's white paint. I couldn't see into the cab. Thinking McKay was hurt, I took out my phone to call 911.

The passenger door of the pickup rose. A black duffel bag sailed out, dropped to the ground. McKay followed the duffel bag. He snatched it and headed across the drained rice paddy. I put the phone away and ran down the grade. My feet crunched pebbly dirt. McKay's gait had a hitch to it; he'd been injured in the crash. I reached flat ground.

The pistol, in McKay's right hand, swung with his strides. The duffel bag in his left hand slowed him.

Before reaching the incline at the end of the paddy, McKay turned, aimed and fired. I kept sprinting. McKay dropped the duffel bag and took hold of the pistol with both hands. He aimed the gun at me and fired. He fired again.

I ignored the shots.

McKay snatched the duffel bag and pushed his way up the incline. With him starting from a dead stop, I had the momentum, and he had to swing the duffel bag with each stride.

McKay must have heard me getting close, because he turned around, lowered himself. I was thirty feet away. McKay dropped the duffel bag. He stretched his right arm forward, locked those cat's eyes on mine and fired twice. The shots were explosive noises, nothing more. When I was twenty feet from McKay he fired again. I never stopped running.

McKay looked at the gun. He dropped it. He took steps up the grade, limping, still clutching the duffel bag. McKay spun again and swung at me. My left arm took his fist blow just as my hands coiled around McKay's throat.

I squeezed as hard as I could. Remembering how he'd slammed me down, I kicked one of his feet off the ground and drove him back-first onto slanted earth. My circled hands squeezed like wringing water from a towel. My thumbs jammed into his windpipe. I banged McKay's head into the ground, over and over and over. McKay didn't have a chance to regain his wits. His life was a struggle for air. I went crazy. It was as if killing McKay would somehow bring Clyde Whitney back, like I could trade the one for the other.

Each time I banged McKay's head into the ground brought a thumping sound.

"Enough! Jeff! Enough!"

Naugle's voice.

"Jeff! I've cuffed his ankles. Let go!"

Two hands gripped the back of my shirt. I was pulled off of Dennis McKay. I rolled left, took out my knife and snapped open its blade. I kicked the duffel bag aside.

McKay's hands clung to his throat. He coughed rather than breathed. His usually piercing eyes were hazy as a drunk's waking to find himself on the sidewalk. They looked blankly upward.

Greg Naugle, on hands and knees, breathing hard and coughing himself, pointed to McKay's feet. A set of handcuffs locked the ankles together.

I nodded. I crawled to McKay, yanked off both tennis shoes and threw them in opposite directions.

Naugle was too out of breath to speak.

McKay was too out of breath to speak.

I stood, walked away from McKay, still on his back, and brandished the switchblade. McKay's eyes remained blank as he clutched his throat and coughed between quick hoarse breaths.

Naugle crawled to McKay. He jerked McKay's hands overhead. McKay was too dazed to really fight but he brought his hands down. Naugle pulled a length of yellow nylon rope from a back pocket, seized McKay's wrists again and tied them together with the swiftness of a rodeo cowboy. He cinched the rope tight. McKay yelped. His eyes scrunched closed.

Naugle crawled away from him.

Across the rice paddy, at the dirt road, a car engine came to life. Naugle and I looked up to see the Jetta spurt forward, leaving a stream of smoky dust.

Twenty-four

I grabbed the black duffel bag and towed Naugle away from McKay. We sat high up on the incline. I took out my phone, called Clint and asked him to tell the sheriff's office I had a suspect in the death Clyde Whitney waiting for them.

Clint said, "That should get them moving."

We both clicked off.

I said, "Where'd the cuffs come from?"

Naugle said, "Every once in a while, you get a wild one at a fire. We got to act before the police arrive. Since I'm always on call, I carry a pair in the car. Also rope, gas masks, the whole nine yards."

McKay turned and looked up the slope. I waved the knife. "You try to free your hands, you get this. You can't run, anyway."

"Fuck you."

McKay's words sounded like they washed over gravel. I'd done a number on his throat. I did not regret it.

I said, "Calder told me what you did to Clyde Whitney. How you told him you were taking him to heaven, led him to the pond and drowned him."

McKay's raspy words cuffed the air. "That lying sack of shit. He was in it the whole time. He even made a joke about leading a horse to water."

"Tell your story to the police."

McKay lay back. He closed his eyes. What could he do? His ankles were confined. He had no shoes, his wrists were bound. He said, "I just got it. That asshole's gun was all blanks." McKay turned his neck side to side. He made no attempt to stand. "How'd you get out? Did I miss a side tunnel?"

"Calder unscrewed the thing. He's strong as a bull."

My phone pinged. I pulled it out, clicked.

Karen said, "Is everything okay?"

The sounds of an approaching vehicle distracted me. I looked in that direction. Flashing blue and red lights.

Karen, in her even-keeled voice: "I asked you if everything is okay."

"Yes. Good enough. I can't really talk now."

A sheriff's department patrol car headed our way. Carrying the duffel bag, I stepped up the incline to the flat road. I set the bag down. I looked back to be sure McKay didn't attempt to go after Naugle. A male officer drove the black-and-white cruiser.

The deputy emerged hatless. His hair was brown and cut like a marine's. Large of frame, forties, his jowls jiggled as he approached. He said something into a tiny microphone pinned to his shirt pocket. It barked back numbers at him.

He said, "I got a call about a murder suspect."

I pointed to the drained rice paddy, empty except for a white pickup truck on its side, a pistol in the dirt, and two men on the incline, one standing, one prone.

The deputy said, "I assume the one tied up." He unsnapped his holster and drew his service revolver. He pointed. "That gun been fired?"

I said, "Six times. But its shells were blanks."

"Blanks?"

"Saved my life."

The deputy kept his gun drawn. "I'm Deputy Sousa. Who are you?"

"Jeff Taylor."

"You got some explaining to do. Save it till the lieutenant arrives."

I called to Naugle, "How about if you join us up here?"

Lieutenant Burns arrived in a different unmarked car than the first time we'd crossed paths. He climbed out, hitched up his navy blue slacks and headed for Deputy Sousa, who watched over the three of us with the drawn gun. Burns wore a white shirt and thin purple tie that flapped as he walked. No overcoat, no gun. By the time he reached us, his black shoes were covered with dust.

Deputy Sousa gave him a crisp salute. Burns ignored Sousa.

To me, he said, "Clint Sherman claims you have a murder suspect for me." He gestured toward McKay. "I assume that's him."

"That is correct."

"By what authority do you have him tied and handcuffed?"

"He's tied and handcuffed because he tried to lock me and another man in an underground bomb shelter. As in he tried to kill us. He stole gold dust from the deceased Clyde Whitney." I picked up the black duffel back and set it closer to Lieutenant Burns. "And he shot at me six times."

McKay sat up. He looked flustered, like maybe he had a concussion. He said, "They were blanks."

"You didn't know they were blanks. You tried to kill me."

"They were blanks, man. You're the one who shot at me first."

"I never shot at you."

Burns said, "That's enough. Both of you. You answer questions, but that's it."

Finally, he recognized Deputy Sousa's presence. "Well?"

Sousa pointed to the gun. "That's it down there. I didn't touch it."

Burns scratched his forehead. He took a couple of steps down the incline. "Whose truck is that?"

McKay said, "It's mine."

"How'd it end up on its side?"

"That asshole slashed the left tires, then the fucker chased me for no reason."

Burns raised his right hand. "Easy on the language, mister. By the way, what's your name?"

"Dennis McKay."

"From?"

"Folsom."

"I'll get to you in a minute." Burns turned to me. "Tell me about this underground bomb shelter."

"Clyde Whitney, who you got fished out of the pond in Crystal Meadows, had a gold mine on a river island farther down this road. Over the years, he stored his findings in an old bomb shelter no one else knew about. As he got near the end of his life, people began wondering where he'd put his gold all these years. Including me. You may remember I'm attached to Clyde Whitney's granddaughter."

"I said tell me about the bomb shelter."

"I learned of its existence this morning. I came to check it out. McKay was already in there with a man, first name of Calder. They'd scooped up the gold you'll find in the bag. McKay had tied up Calder before I arrived. That's when he fired his first shot. He left me and Calder underground, thinking he'd locked us down there. But we got out."

Burns raised his right hand again, for quiet. "Are you Calder?"

"I'm Greg Naugle. Stockton Fire."

"You got ID confirming that?"

Naugle reached for his back pocket.

Burns said, "Show me later. Where is this Calder?"

I said, "When I chased McKay in my car, he crashed." I pointed to the white pickup on its side. Smoke still rose from under the hood. "I went after him. He fired at me five times, not knowing the gun contained only blanks. It's Calder's gun, by the way. When Captain Naugle and myself were subduing this guy," I said, motioning to Dennis McKay, "Calder stole my car."

Burns looked to Naugle.

Naugle said, "That's true."

This time Burns scratched his chin. He looked to Sousa. "Does any of this make sense to you?"

"I don't know, sir."

Burns turned his attention to Dennis McKay. McKay went to stand up. Burns said, "You stay down. Tell me what you know about the disappearing Calder."

"His name's Calder Crayon."

Burns said, "Seriously?"

McKay said, "He's an ex jockey. He lives with a well-known horse trainer, RaeLynn Davidson, down in New Mexico."

"What is your association with Mr. Crayon?"

McKay tossed Burns one of his sneers. "I just gave you the name of Whitney's murderer. Other than that, not a word till I talk to my lawyer."

Without glancing at Sousa, Burns said, "Put that gun away." He looked off, in thought.

The five of us were out in the sun on the edge of a drained rice paddy, land that held nothing but weeds, dead grass and an overturned pickup truck. Burns' eyes caught sight of something. Four of us looked north. McKay, on the ground, continued to stare into sky.

Columns of dust rose behind two cars. In front was Karen's dusky Volvo. Close behind was Clint Sherman's black Lexus SUV. Burns' right hand returned to his forehead. He stared at the approaching vehicles.

McKay hollered to him: "Calder killed Whitney. Not me. I won't let the screwy hand guy pin anything on me."

Burns looked at me. I showed him my mangled hand. Burns walked down to Dennis McKay. He looked at McKay's red face, his scraped neck, his hands and feet bound. McKay ventured an arrogant smile.

Burns said, "My neighbor's daughter has a bum leg. She falls down when playing on the lawn with my kids. You want to make a crack about her next? You like making fun of people who have a rough start in life?"

McKay said, "Get me my lawyer. His card is in my wallet."

Burns stepped up to the lip of the rice paddy. He said to Deputy Sousa, "When somebody you're questioning carries his lawyer's business card around, it qualifies as a red flag. You keep after him until you get answers you believe."

"Yes, sir."

The two vehicles stopped by the patrol car, and the unmarked county car, with Naugle's red Subaru parked sideways beyond them. Clint and Karen got out of their cars, exchanged words and shook hands. They walked toward the rest of us. I noted Karen slowed so Clint could keep up.

Clint waved. He called ahead. "John."

Burns called back. "Clint."

Both nodded. For the moment, that was it between them.

Karen and Clint reached us. She wore her sky-blue nurse's uniform and white nursing shoes.

I said, "Karen, this is Greg Naugle."

190

They shook hands.

He said, "Nice to meet you."

Karen said the same.

I reached an arm toward Clint. Though tall and physically active, his seventy-six years and the trifocals reflecting sunlight showed his age.

To Naugle, I said, "Clint Sherman."

Clint and Naugle shook hands.

I pointed downhill to McKay. "That's Dennis McKay. The first guy who followed me, and ran me off the road."

McKay raised his arms as best he could, and flipped us two birds through the rope tying his hands together.

To Naugle, I said, "This is Deputy Sousa." I gestured to Burns. "Lieutenant Burns, county police."

Naugle said it was nice to meet him.

Burns said, "What the hell is this, a meet and greet?"

"What this is," Clint said, "is a private citizen finishing up your work."

Burns said, "I decide when the work is finished."

Clint said, "Let's you and I go to your car. Get out of this sun. I'll fill you in on what you've been missing."

Irritated, Burns walked toward the unmarked police car. After a dozen steps, he stopped, and waited for Clint to catch up. Burns surveyed the group, the white truck on its side, and took in the whole of the drained rice paddy.

Burns said, "When Mr. Sherman and I return, you're all going down to the station to make signed statements."

Deputy Sousa said, "Yes, sir."

Lieutenant Burns shook his head. "They will be making signed statements. You will be making a signed *report*."

"Yes, sir."

At reaching Burns, Clint gave him a gentle pat on the shoulder. "Let's get out of this sun."

Karen, Naugle and I sat on dirt and made small talk. Sousa kept an eye on McKay. His gun rested in its holster. The holster remained unsnapped. Karen told Naugle what she was studying in graduate school. Naugle described his role in the Stockton fire department. I asked him a couple of questions. In the midst of all that craziness, we talked like three people wanting to get to know each other.

Karen said, "Once we finish with the police, we should check on Rattlesnake. Just to be sure those guys didn't mess with him."

I said, "I was thinking the same thing."

Naugle said, "I'd be interested in meeting someone named Rattlesnake."

I said, "Don't get alarmed if he comes out of his cabin and starts waving a Winchester rifle."

Naugle said, "Good to know."

Twenty-five

Discussion involving me was surely part of Clint and Lieutenant Burns' twenty minutes in the unmarked police car. I'd withheld evidence. I'd stolen gold. I'd threatened and without provocation fired a gun toward an unarmed man. The police had reasons to make me squirm, at least in the short term. I figured Clint had something valuable to trade, because after I made a complete statement at the sheriff's office I was not charged, or threatened to be charged, with anything.

It was almost six when Karen, Naugle and I signed papers and walked outside together. We hadn't seen Dennis McKay and had no clues about what was happening to him. Karen invited Naugle to join us for dinner. He said no thanks. Drained from the day's action, his steps were slow. We shook hands and said goodbye.

Karen and I left in her Volvo. She drove. We thought we should check on Rattlesnake. I called an ex-teammate, Nick Hopper. We'd played two years together at Sacramento State. Nick went on to become a hotshot lawyer down in Laguna Beach. I gave him the details I thought mattered most, and asked for advice. The conversation lasted until we reached the bridge to Genoa Island. I was surprised there was no yellow police tape. Since no one could advance without the code, Burns probably thought it could wait until the next day.

SCOTT LIPANOVICH

Karen and I crossed the bridge. We passed the gate as it clanged against the side rail. The gate began its slow, groaning return trip to being shut.

I said, "How dumb do you think I can be? To not think of something."

Karen said, "Taylor, the possibilities are endless."

"Clyde said, 'The ceiling at heaven is golden.'"

"Been there, done that."

"We haven't. Calder told me about collecting baggies all around the floor, and in the cabinets. He didn't say anything about the ceiling."

"If there was some kind of weird net, you would've seen it."

"That is correct. But if your grandfather has been hiding his gold all these years, before he started dropping things, maybe there's a ceiling compartment in the bomb shelter. I didn't notice one, but I was busy staying alive. I went at least twelve feet underground. The ceiling was about eight feet high."

Karen shook her head. "It's stubborn-mule time."

She drove over dead grass. We reached the digger pines forest, parked where I'd parked in the morning. I took two flashlights and the toolbox from the trunk of the Volvo. A desert-like scent floated in the breeze blowing down the Feather River and across the southern end of Genoa Island. We went to the still open bomb shelter.

Karen said, "If I go down there with you, and we don't find anything, you owe me big time."

"Put it on my bill."

We scoured the steel ceiling of the bomb shelter. It was made of four-by-eight feet rectangles welded together. There was nothing to slide open, nothing to pry or anything to gain access to above.

Karen sat at the steel table in the eating area, near the sink. She

194

shined her flashlight around. The flashlights I'd left on the table in the morning had died. Karen said, "This whole thing is bizarre. You couldn't live in here long enough for radiation outside to be at a safe level. Not by months."

I said, "People thought the end was coming. They got desperate."

Karen shined her flashlight at me, found my face. "What do I get for following you on this goose chase?"

"A goose dinner."

Karen said, "I was thinking more along the lines of season tickets to the symphony."

I gave up on the ceiling. I went around the wall of labeled, partly open cabinets. I searched the ceiling there. I detected nothing of note. I thought the sides of the lower stairwell might be a place to store gold but again, nothing.

Coming down the stairs, shining the flashlight most everywhere, I saw a small thin rectangle in the steel, upper left corner of the wall backing the cabinets. It was about eighteen inches below the ceiling. Running the light left to right, I saw another rectangle dead center, then another rectangle on the right end of the wall.

I reached up and pushed on the one to the left. It gave, though there was resistance. I slowly pushed the square of metal inward, then turned it on its side and angled it out. I was doused with half-filled Ziploc baggies of gold dust.

From the other side of the wall: "What was that?"

I said, "You see the two buckets stacked by the sink?"

Karen must have shined her light toward the sink. "What about them?"

"If you bring them over here, we can start loading up a fortune."

Dusk settled over the island as we finished packing the contents of the three compartments into Karen's Volvo. We decided it was too late to show up at Rattlesnake's without warning.

*

Plodding our way on the clogged freeway toward Crystal Meadows, I called Stan Whitney.

"We need to talk. Privately, just the two of us."

"When?"

"Give me an hour. Karen and I are stuck on Highway 80. This needs to be just the two of us. It involves your family, and the future."

"I think I understand. I'll meet you at the main back door at nine-thirty. No need to ring the bell."

Stan didn't mention any communication with the police. He didn't seem the least hesitant or uncomfortable.

At Karen's guesthouse I took a quick shower, wolfed down bread and cheese, threw on a fresh dark T-shirt and made it to the back of the Whitney McMansion at nine-thirty. Stan summoned me in. His handshake was insistent, his smile bright, his blond hair so solid I thought if I knocked on it, I could ring out a tune. His half undone scarlet tie seemed designed to show he was an industrious, yet relaxed businessman.

Stan said, "Laura's upstairs watching *Antiques Roadshow*. Let's do this in the map space."

I followed Stan through the back dining room, and the great room, to a den office twice the size of my living room. Stan motioned for me to take one of two tan leather chairs substantial enough to accommodate Sumo wrestlers. The leather was soft as butter.

Stan, on the other side of a table with slots holding what I guessed were real estate maps, leaned forward. He rubbed his palms together. "Before you start, I want to say I think things between you and Karen have moved awfully fast. No offense, but that's how it seems from my vantage point."

Not prepared for that, I looked around and wondered how I'd change the conversation to murder and thievery. "I agree with you."

Stan smiled. Perhaps I'd pleased him. He said, "As I'm sure Karen told you, her father has been out of the picture for more than a decade. They don't communicate at all."

"That's my understanding."

Stan seemed never to need to think about what came next. "I take it as a compliment you want to have this talk. Now that my father's gone, I'm the only male figure in Karen's life who is a blood relative. With Karen's father nothing but absent, I feel an obligation to look out for her best interests."

I thought: He thinks *that*?

I played Stan like a fish on the line. "And what do you see as her best interests?"

"First off, you being in medical school is a positive. At the same time, you and Karen have only known each other about six weeks."

I nodded. "Wednesday will be six weeks."

Stan walked right into it.

"Until Karen finishes her masters, and you at least get a residency, I can't give you my blessing. I'm confident my sisters will agree."

I stood, walked around the room. On the walls were framed maps of real estate developments. In most I caught the emblem *Whitney Properties, Inc.* From a back pocket I took my copy of the statement I'd given to the police, three single-spaced typed pages, stapled, now folded into thirds like a letter.

I handed the pages to Stan. I sat on a leather throne. "You need to read this. It'll get us to why we have to talk."

Stan gave a half shrug. He unfolded the typed statement, began reading. Not far in, he darted to a credenza and took out a pair of reading glasses. He didn't sit. He stayed near the polished wood credenza, and read. By the time he was on page three, his cheeks were bright pink. He finished reading. He set the glasses down. His cerulean blue eyes popped with anger.

"You son of a bitch."

I said, "That's fair. But there are a few sons of bitches in this. Hal Bell was after Clyde's gold. You hired Dennis McKay to investigate me, and make things so I'd back away from seeing Karen."

"I was protecting my niece from a gold digger." He slapped my typed statement as if proving his claim.

I said, "You're a son of a bitch because you hired the man who murdered your dad. Think about it. You call me a son of a bitch. Fine. What does hiring the man who murdered your father make you?"

A surprise: Stan was overwhelmed. There was no place in the conversation for his endless patter and sales pitches. He sat in the other leather throne. He did not seem sad. Stan said, "What do you want?"

"Don't worry, you'll come out fine."

"What do you mean by 'fine'? McKay's going to go to trial. Me hiring him is going to make the papers, along with everything that transpired. I have a reputation in this state."

I said, "That's not of interest to me."

Stan's face seemed to acquire new hues of red. No home runs for him that night. He said, "I'll ask you again. What do you want?"

I said, "Everybody knows you're the executor of your father's estate."

"What about it?"

"I want you to agree to your sisters hiring a third party, known to none of the principals. To make sure everything is divided evenly."

That brought a smile, and a twinkle to Stan's blazing eyes. "Why would I do that? I've managed dad's affairs for years. Quite lucratively."

"It's simple. If you don't agree to this, I'll sue the estate, sue the trusts, anything your name is attached to. I'll tie up your businesses for years. Think about the interviews I'll give the newspapers. There are things in that statement I can expand on. Like what it was like to be trapped underground by someone you sent envelopes to containing hundred dollar bills."

"You son of a bitch."

"Now, if you'll excuse me, I'm going to go help Karen pack."

Stan's mouth opened. He looked up. His ears joined his cheeks in growing redness. "I was right about you."

"I was right about you."

I snatched the police statement pages from Stan. I left the room. Stan followed me into the great room.

"Hey, Jeff. One question."

I stopped.

"If I went along with this, how do I know you won't eventually go to the press? Maybe sue me personally, not the estate, after Dad's assets get divided."

"How do I know you won't hire another thug to pound me?"

Karen didn't have much to pack. It fit in her car, as on her drive West, though with me and her school materials it was a tight squeeze. Away from the city, stars splashed across the night sky.

I said, "Will you moving out cause a rift between Stan and your mom?"

"Me moving in with you, no. What we did getting Grandpa's gold, yes. You trying to force Uncle Stan into getting an outside source to handle the estate? If it works, my mom's going to love you for it. So will Aunt Lila."

We put Karen's things in the second bedroom, ate a late meal. We fell asleep in each other's arms.

Early in the morning, Karen and I were awakened by my phone. I rolled onto a side, toward the end table. I answered the phone.

Lieutenant Burns identified himself, and said, "Your vehicle has been recovered. Not a scratch."

"Good news. And thanks." I shook cobwebs from my head. "What about Crayon?"

"We got him. Two fifteen a.m., the Sacramento Hilton."

"Are you allowed to give me the details?"

Burns laughed. It was the only time he hadn't seemed glum or pushy in our exchanges. "The dummy goes to the hotel where his girlfriend's staying. Parks your car right behind hers. When officers determine the room, knock and demand they open up, Crayon hides in a closet."

My mind clearing, I pictured little muscle man Calder Crayon scooting into darkness, staying still like a child playing hide and seek. I said, "The man's an odd duck. So's Aunty Rae."

"Aunty Rae?"

Karen poked me in the back. She whispered, "Aunty Rae?"

I pointed to the phone, spread my thumb and forefinger an inch apart, indicating I needed a minute.

I said to Burns, "That's what RaeLynn Davidson goes by. She's Clyde Whitney's niece."

"That's rich. Anyway, the officers threaten to force the door. Ms. Davidson flings it open. She swings an ashtray at the first officer. His partner tries to subdue her without undue force, and she kicks him hard as hell in the shins. She's put on cowboy boots with steel toe caps. She's in the boots, a see-through nightgown and hair curlers. She's screaming, 'Go away! Leave my Crayon

200

alone! Leave my Crayon alone!' Over and over as they cuff her. She's wearing the curlers in her mug shot. That much quality entertainment in police work doesn't come along often."

"Sounds like a good time was had by all."

"Not by Mr. Crayon. He's piling up offenses."

After that, Burns told me I'd have to wait for the Jetta till the fingerprint technician finished her work. Then I'd go fill out a form, and the car was mine again.

"Thanks. Good work by the police."

Silence. Silence long enough I thought Burns hung up and I hadn't had a chance to describe to him my return visit to the bomb shelter.

I was about to click off when Burns said, "Jeff, you did a lot of wrong here."

"I know I did."

He said, "I'm not sure what course the D.A. will want to take. I'll recommend no charges be filed against you for holding McKay against his will, and reckless behavior with the gunshot out on the street. Taking the gold is between you and the Whitney family, considering Ms. Brady's participation."

I said, "Speaking of gold, I have something for you."

"Yeah?"

"Approximately a million dollars in gold dust. I'll swing by with it later on today."

Burns said, "You'll meet me here at nine sharp."

Twenty-six

I called Clint and thanked him for the day before.

"What did you say to Burns? He's not exactly friendly, but he clearly wants to keep me out of trouble."

"We had a friendly chat. I mentioned a rumor regarding business deals involving a certain member of the planning commission. He's using a false front for investments in midtown condo conversions he voted be granted zoning changes. He'll make a pile. John Burns is at that stage in life he'd like to be referred to as Council Member Burns. Busting the guy will make a big splash. You don't mention this to anyone."

Next, I called Dr. Fisher, to tell him I'd be late. He said, flatly, "See you then."

I dropped Karen at the medical center, then headed to the sheriff's department. Burns was not chatty. He gave me a receipt that detailed what was received. I drove to the medical center. In Dr. Fisher's office, I handed him the copy of my statement. I said I was going to the cafeteria for orange juice.

When I returned, Dr. Fisher swung the computer screen away from in front of him. He motioned for me to sit in the chair Clyde Whitney sat in the day we'd met.

Dr. Fisher rubbed his eyes. They tended to tire from staring at a computer screen. He said, "You've had an adventurous time since starting here. I had no idea."

"I didn't give you that police statement as an excuse. It's more like going to traffic court, and pleading guilty with an explanation."

Dr. Fisher nodded. "I guess," he said, lifting the signed pages on his desk, "you live in the fast lane, whereas I'm still horse and buggy."

I said, "It's been more like a roller coaster."

Dr. Fisher folded his hands and set them on his desk. He said, "I can't pretend your poor attendance, and last-second failures to show up didn't happen. They'll be in the summary I make of your time here. The reason I won't hide it is from the time that McKay ran you down, you could have contacted the authorities. Also, you kept stolen gold dust in this building."

"It's still here."

"You're reinforcing my point. But my main point is, any physician who decides to make up his or her own rules will inevitably cause harm to patients."

"I understand."

Dr. Fisher swung the computer screen to in front of him. He tapped keys, read the screen. He said, "Let's check on Oppenheim's patient. He called to say he'll be out of town till Monday. He's at a golf tournament in Boise. That man's a terrific golfer."

On the way, Dr. Fisher said, "I've wondered, but didn't want to get personal. Do you still miss playing?"

"I play in my dreams. Sometimes I rack up points. Sometimes the basket moves sideways when I shoot. Or my hand falls off. Yes, I miss it. Would you indulge me in telling you my most recent basketball dream?"

"I've been indulging you for weeks."

"You got me there. Anyway, a couple nights ago, I dreamed I'm playing in a packed gym. Everybody's screaming. I dribble down the court. The noise is so intense the gym floor vibrates through my shoes. When I wake up, my feet are buzzing like in the dream. I walk to the living room. They're still buzzing. This goes on for about five minutes."

We reached the patient's room. Dr. Fisher, normally a straightforward person, became enigmatic: "Lucky you."

Twenty-seven

I met Clyde Whitney because he had lung cancer and was driven once a week to radiation treatments by a friend. Once a week I drove Greg Naugle to radiation treatments. The first few Tuesdays, he invited me in to meet his wife, Maureen, and son, Mark; daughter Amy was at Arizona State. I always wiggled out of going inside the house. I think it was because I didn't want to share what little time I'd have with my dad with anyone. Naugle's wife and I did talk on the phone about his condition, which worsened. The final blow came when a scan revealed the cancer had spread to his brain.

During the drives to and from Stockton General Hospital, we didn't talk much. At first this felt odd. Eventually, it became comforting. It was our way.

Naugle became much thinner. He weaved when he walked. I'd take him by the elbow and guide him from the car into the hospital, and down its halls. Always polite, thankful, he never uttered a word of complaint or self-pity. His mind faded. It got so he had to be reminded of my name. Twice he confused me with Mark.

Two weeks after Greg Naugle died, I wrote a letter to Mark Naugle. I invited him to meet me at Ryder Channing Park, in downtown Sacramento. I pointed out that was where his dad and I first met.

I didn't burden Mark with reminding him of how fine a person his father was. I didn't convey feelings of loss, or pride, because Mark was sixteen years old and the last thing he'd want is to get touchy-feely. He had plenty of emotions to deal with on his own.

I gave Mark my email address. I wrote that weekdays I was swamped, but on a Saturday or Sunday morning I'd appreciate it if he'd drive the forty-five miles north and shoot baskets with me.

A week later, I received a message: *Saturday morning at 9:00.*

I replied: *Bring a ball if possible. I will too.*

Mark turned out to be a younger version of Greg Naugle. Six feet, a little on the thin side, his hazel eyes burned with the intensity of adolescence. He'd gotten a feel for the hoop by coming early. I liked that. He wore a green T-shirt with *Saint Mary's Rams* printed across the front in white, green basketball shorts, and fancy basketball shoes I knew nothing about. We exchanged hellos. We didn't shake hands. No one else was on the courts that early. The sounds of two balls bouncing on asphalt ruled the airwaves. It reminded me of good times. Mark had chosen a basket with the sun slowly climbing behind us.

Before taking a shot, he said, "My dad said you were a star." He fired away from fifteen feet. The ball bounced off the rim. Mark loped after it.

"I never ran into burning buildings to save people."

Mark dribbled the ball back onto the court. He said, "I looked up Sac. State basketball. You still hold most of the records."

I'd been dribbling but had not taken a shot. Off and on, after my hand got chopped, I'd tried shooting left handed. I never got good at it from more than a dozen feet. I'd improvised a clunky set shot, where my stubbed right hand pushed the ball up and out, kind of like someone throws the shot put. I gave it a try. It went in.

206

I said, "Pure luck."

Mark did some fancy dribbling and popped in a fifteen footer. He went to the net, slapped the ball after one bounce, dribbled to the top of the key. "Want to go one-on-one? I don't care who wins."

"You'd wipe me out. Besides, the hand can't take a lot of getting knocked into. Want to play Around The World?"

Mark gave me a smart-ass laugh. "That's for kids."

Dribbling, I picked up the ball, held it against my stomach. "I have no trouble conceding I can't play full go anymore. You don't have to rub it in."

Mark's face darkened. He looked down, reminding me of his dad. "I'm sorry."

I said, "Let's shoot. Around The World. You go first."

Mark was more accurate than expected. As he advanced, making his shots and me bounce-passing the ball to him, I recognized our resemblance. Mark wasn't only a younger version of his dad, he was a shorter version of me at sixteen. He finally missed. My turn.

We shot baskets for an hour. After, we agreed to meet again the next Saturday, at Victory Park in Stockton.

Mark said, "My court." He grinned. "Bring a few bucks."

We shot hoops every Saturday. In October, when sister Amy flew home for a weekend, she joined in. Maureen called that afternoon.

"I don't know how much is your influence, how much is time, but Mark's focused again. Straight As in school. Basketball every afternoon. He keeps saying they're going to win league."

"Anything I contributed is because of a man named Clyde Whitney, who I believe was an American saint."

I heard Maureen blow her nose. She said, "Whatever. Just thanks, okay?"

Twenty-eight

In all, one-point-four million dollars' worth of Clyde's gold dust was recovered, depending on a day's market value. After the police completed their investigation, Karen and I locked up the bomb shelter, covered it with a mound of dirt that we planted with native grass seeds. Then we enjoyed a celebratory lunch with Rattlesnake Johnson.

He said, "Clyde sure beat the skeptics. No surprise here."

I never saw nor spoke with Hal Bell again. Dennis McKay went to jail for murder and other offenses, twenty-seven years, eligible for parole in half that. Calder Crayon got sixteen years, possible parole in eight. He claimed Aunty Rae knew nothing about Clyde's death. That was likely nonsense but there was no way to prove she knew. She got a fine and two hundred hours of community service for resisting arrest and assaulting a police officer. The court agreed to allow Aunty Rae to meet her obligations out of state. One day a week she opened her stables to an organization that worked with underprivileged kids in Albuquerque. She gave riding lessons, and instruction in horse grooming and ranch management. She kept Karen up to date on this; Karen was the only family member who took her calls. Every month Aunty Rae flew to California for her allotted visit with Calder Crayon. We declined her invitations to lunch.

Stan Whitney didn't fight a third party handling Clyde's estate and trusts. He was boxed in by my threat to file lawsuits and make calls to newspapers. Plus, McKay's court testimony pushed Stan into keeping a low profile.

No charges were filed against Stan, as McKay had quit working for him before Clyde was murdered.

We couldn't prove Calder stole the three baggies of gold dust from my place, and decided it wasn't worth further muddying the waters of our own behavior by trying to.

Karen and I never determined who broke into Clyde's house. My candidate was Dennis McKay.

Rattlesnake had said Clyde was a secretive soul. When working in satellite technology, he was known for doing complex math computations in his head and revealing only the answers. With gold extraction, drawings for buildings and water pipe systems were found, and not a sentence describing his method. Clyde took that with him to wherever he went after passing on.

Late November, on a Friday night, Karen and I drove through rain to Saint Mary's High School, in Stockton, to watch the season's first game. I didn't tell Mark or Maureen because I didn't want him to be self-conscious. We sat high on the opponent's side. Mark didn't score many points. He passed the ball to teammates rather than take quick shots, covered for them when they got beat on defense, dove to the floor for every loose ball. In the last minutes, the game played below me in slow motion. I saw the seams of the gently spinning basketball. The beauty of the evolving game, its intricacies and simplicities, were laid out for me as if on a ninety-foot table. I knew what was going to happen just before it happened. It was like the best moments of my own time in the sport.

Karen tapped my knee. She leaned over, spoke into my ear to be heard over cheering. "You're enthralled."

I said, "Watch Mark. He plays with his heart. He holds nothing back."

Her breath had a distinct scent: Karen Brady. It was as unmistakable as the scent of the virgin redwood forest where I used to fall into the trance of my mind game, Disappear. Karen's scent mixed with shouts in the crowd, bouncing ball sounds, the smell of popcorn, the squeaking of tennis shoes cutting across the hardwood court.

Karen tapped me on the knee again. "We're getting season tickets. I don't mean the symphony."

About the Author

Scott Lipanovich lives in Santa Rosa, California. Stories of his have appeared in *Ireland's Fish Story Prize*, *The Seattle Review*, *Crosscurrents*, *Defiant Scribe*, *Abiko* (Japan), *Wild Duck Review*, *Ridge Review*, *Gold and Treasure Hunter Magazine*, *Summerfield Journal*, and several anthologies. In film, he has worked with two Academy Award winners, and two multiple Emmy-winning producers.

Scott is the author of the Jeff Taylor Mysteries, *The Lost Coast* (Encircle, July 2021), and *The Golden Ceiling*. Book three, *Sky Lake*, will be published in 2023.

If you enjoyed reading this book,
please consider writing your honest review
and sharing it with other readers.

Many of our Authors are happy to participate in
Book Club and Reader Group discussions.
For more information, contact us at info@encirclepub.com.

Thank you,
Encircle Publications

For news about more exciting new fiction, join us at:

Facebook: www.facebook.com/encirclepub

Instagram: www.instagram.com/encirclepublications

Twitter: twitter.com/encirclepub

Sign up for Encircle Publications newsletter and specials:
eepurl.com/cs8taP